ALL-AMERICAN
APHRODITE

DANIEL LYONS

ALL-AMERICAN APHRODITE

iUniverse books may be ordered through booksellers or by contacting:

iUniverse
1663 Liberty Drive
Bloomington, IN 47403
www.iuniverse.com
1-800-Authors (1-800-288-4677)

ISBN: 978-1-5320-5677-2 (sc)
ISBN: 978-1-5320-5678-9 (e)

Library of Congress Control Number: 2018912134

Print information available on the last page.

iUniverse rev. date: 02/21/2019

For Mark Lester

CHAPTER ONE

At this point in the evening, the hotel room smells, as ever, a bit like rotten fish. It is a paradox typical of the universe, Senator Milton Bergman has speculated many times, that the most pleasant things in life must always be juxtaposed with the least pleasant. The most objectionable. As though there truly were a string directly connecting all opposites, a string that does not exist between things that are merely similar or dissimilar from one another. Perhaps the very balance, and with it the existence, of the universe depends on such strings as these, holding it all together.

The room is a pricey affair, as is to be expected of a senator's trysting place, sprawling, luxurious. Marble, porcelain, thick green carpet, dark red velvet drapes, oak paneling, king-size bed complete with flowery patterns on the sheets and pillowcases. A writing desk, polished wood, several lamps, all shaded, brightly white.

A bathroom nearly as large as the bedroom. Five stars for the shower alone.

And in the middle of it, the girl, the most expensive component of all, the goddess herself, specifically toned by Larsen's Reproductions along with thousands of others to provide the market with the most satisfactory range of bodies possible. She lies in the center of the bed, in the center of the room, surprisingly close to the center of the hotel—the front half at least, the side facing the ocean, viewable through the ten feet of french doors leading out onto the marbled terrace.

The wizards at Larsen's might have had Senator Bergman specifically in mind when they crafted this girl into what she is now. Who knows what she may have been once? That is the miracle of Larsen's. They can do anything, and you would never know. Ole Larsen figured out how to work his way around silicone and how to utilize chemicals that change how the body distributes fat, builds up muscles, pigments the skin, everything. The word was made flesh, and the flesh was made to please—to please oneself, to please the senator, you name it.

Milton's tastes run toward the fleshy, the strong, the curvy, the muscular, and—he would blush to admit to some of his constituents—toward his fellow Caucasians, though he has bedded all kinds. He does not like them pale; he prefers a tan, a soft tan, a perfect tan, as though the skin were naturally bronze.

So she is, the girl Fantasies Inc. has ordered to call herself Atalanta. She lies facedown on the bed now, snoozing off their mutual exercise, her muscular backside hunched ever so slightly in the air, the curve of it gleaming in the lamplight like a crescent moon. Dark brown hair spills over her lighter brown shoulders. The fulsomeness of her flesh belies the strength, the muscularity beneath it. Soft and firm at the same time, everywhere.

He is half-asleep himself, sitting deep in the leather swivel chair behind the writing desk, watching her sleep. The cold breath exhaled from his nostrils drifts across the sweat dripping from his chest hair, startling him back toward wakefulness. Perhaps it would be wise to join her in sleep, keep up his strength for the next round, but he loves to watch them sleep, especially when they are naked. She had curled up under the covers, in fact, after they finished, maybe expecting him to join her. Instead, he settled himself into the leather chair and rested there, waiting for her to doze off. As soon as her eyelids stopped fluttering, as her breathing became deeper and more regular, he crept over to the bed and pulled the sheet down, until it was down around her knees, offering him his current view.

The smell intensified when he pulled the sheet down, though it was strong enough already. Milton has a very keen sense of smell. The room initially smelled of disinfectant, of cleaning supplies, of wood and leather and tile, naturally, the finest products, so comforting. There was the smell of his laundered suit, the smell of her perfume, of wine, before they disrobed, the smell of deodorant, of her flesh, of musk, after the clothes came off, the smells of bodily fluids and increasingly of sweat. The olfactory dimension was always the best part for Bergman.

Then afterward, the smell of the docks, lost on the girl. It probably would have meant nothing to her, even if she had been awake.

The red digits on the bedside clock inform him that it is a quarter after midnight, shortly before the darkness begins to press upon the edges of his vision and the phantom figures of his thoughts begin to take on solidity and substance. That always happens when sleep is ready to envelop him at last.

Two empty wine bottles sit on the left-hand bedside table, a third on the rightward one, closer to the girl. Green glass drained of red, as thoroughly as he has been drained of come. The taste of the wine is still there in his mouth somewhere, easy to locate, concentrated as ever amid his front teeth and the middle of his tongue. The taste grows strangely bread–like as it congeals, clearly delineated from the more ephemeral traces of Atalanta's sweat, her perfume, her flesh, conveyed there mainly by the tip of his tongue.

Milton settles down on his hip, as close to her as he can get without quite touching her, reaches down, and pulls the sheet up over them both. In so doing, he wraps his arm at last around her shoulders. His fingers curl in her air, and she wriggles closer to him, her ruby lips trembling in the beginnings of some unintelligible murmuring, her eyebrows crinkling together despite the apparent warmth of her reception to his presence.

★ ★ ★

The senator is already asleep by the time she awakens, the clock reading 12:34. Her iPhone is inadvertently hidden behind the wine bottle on the bedside table on her side of the bed.

It is a large bed, but she is a tall, gangly girl with long arms. She does not even need to shift her butt closer to the edge of the bed. She only rolls it over far enough to reach her phone with her outstretched right arm.

The phone briefly blocks out the antiseptic glare of the main overhead light as she raises it high over their intertwined forms. Only then does it occur to her that the sheet is still covering their nakedness. She had the senator fooled at first. She was awake when he pulled the sheet down off her nakedness, but she was truly asleep by the time he climbed into bed with her and pulled it back up.

She edges it down gradually with her feet, kneading them up and down, up and down, cupping the fabric between her toes, until she and the senator are uncovered down to the waist, as much of them as can be captured within the frame of the phone's camera.

Atalanta presses her aquiline nose in as close as she dares to the chiseled jaw of the middle-aged politician, rolls her eyes toward the camera, smiles toothily, and presses her thumb to the white circle at the bottom of the screen.

The first photo gives the world a good look at her breasts, at the senator's burly shoulders and his chest; and so on, down their bodies, until she realizes that despite her best efforts the sheet is still covering their genitals.

Her arm is already growing sore, and sleep is pressing its weight upon her again. Perhaps it is the resulting hurriedness that causes her to start kneading at the sheet again with rather less caution than before. Even so, it seems to be working at first. In fact, it is not until the sheet is creeping down the senator's thigh—and she is judging that she has gone far enough, she is checking the viewfinder and ascertaining that indeed the length of her arm is sufficient for the phone to capture both their faces and the senator's manhood—when the toenails of her right foot scrape across the his left calf, all the way to the ankle.

In the same instant, her heart nearly stops, and her thumb instinctively clenches on the circular button, capturing, among other things, the senator's face precisely as his eyes are on the verge of flickering open out of sleep, into which he has not had time to sink too deeply.

He may not have been sufficiently awake to register the flash, perhaps not even to have registered the full meaning of the clattering sound as she dropped the phone quickly over the side of the bed, all before his eyes were fully open. She does not have time to clear her eyes of guilt and fear—not before he has intuited that all is not well, that this is not a dream, that such noises, such sights, the scent of fear, have no place in an otherwise empty room.

Senator Bergman Arrested in Hotel Scandal
by Natalie Schroder
May 21, 20—

SEATTLE—Senator Milton Bergman, R-WA, was escorted from Seashell Hotel by Seattle police officers shortly after 2:00 a.m., Sunday morning, following a fracas that spurred hotel staff and at least two guests to call 911 in the middle of the night.

Senator Bergman was discovered in the company of an employee of the controversial companion service Fantasies Inc. The companion has been described as a twenty-year-old female brunette by several observers, though Fantasies has refused to disclose her identity. The female in question was not taken into custody, despite Bergman's claims that she was the cause of the upset.

"I have been detained for reasons that have not been properly justified by the Seattle PD," Senator Bergman claimed in the company of his attorney, Alan Marx, who later stated his expectation that the senator will soon be released for lack of evidence.

"The DA's office has nothing," Marx stated. "The senator would be back on the street already if (SPD Chief) Grace Howitzer weren't so desperate for a distraction in the wake of the 'SODO 3' incident last month."

The precise details of the altercation that led to Bergman's arrest remain vague.

"I heard a lot of shouting, what sounded like a lamp breaking, a loud thud, and then the woman started screaming," said Margaret Holmes, a Seashell client who was lodged in the hotel room below Bergman at the time. "That was when I called the cops."

Regardless what explanation the senator might claim to justify his violent behavior, his reasons for being in the company of a Fantasies companion would seem to be less debatable. However, Bergman's attorney has emphatically contradicted the most obvious explanation.

"There is no evidence that Senator Bergman engaged in sexual relations with the woman who was in the room with him when he was detained," Marx insisted when questioned on the subject. "Milton is a faithful husband and a gentleman."

In the absence of the companion in question to testify, it remains an open question, though the Washington voting base may require more convincing.

"I didn't hear them having sex, but they obviously were," Miss Holmes said. "Why else would a girl like that have been in the room?"

Bergman, who has maintained his Senate seat through two terms and four years of a third term as a Republican from a highly Democratic state by toeing a politically moderate line and appealing to the family values of mainstream Christian voters, has spent twenty years building a public image of temperance, abstinence, and moderation. Now the forty-six-year-old senator is facing a public relations disaster.

"If Bergman can serve out the rest of his term without being completely ostracized by the rest of his party, to say nothing of the rest of the government, it will be a miracle," stated Delia Curran, a professor of political science at UW Tacoma. "I'd say the odds are at least five-to-one he is forced to resign within three months."

However, Professor Curran's colleague Jerry Russo, UW Tacoma, offered a rather different assessment when questioned. "If Senator Bergman is pushed to resign, it will not be by the Republican leadership, at least not until the vote has been settled on the upcoming arms bill. President Bohr will not want to see the Republican Party's majority compromised at this juncture, no matter what questions of public relations may arise."

As yet, Senator Bergman seems to have no intention of resigning, nor do his Republican colleagues seem in any hurry to demand it, though several Democratic spokespersons have already issued a call for his resignation.

"This unseemly, violent behavior on the part of a United States senator is beyond unacceptable and must not be tolerated, especially not at this crucial juncture in our nation's societal and legislative development," proclaimed Bergman's colleague, Washington senior Senator Chloe Demetrio, Democrat, who has publicly clashed with Senator Bergman on numerous occasions over the past ten years.

Assuming his own party do not step up to demand Senator Bergman's resignation, it seems unlikely that he will be compelled to leave the Senate before the much-anticipated arms bill vote, scheduled for September, although, as Mr. Russo has implied, the picture may change if the bill passes in the Senate.

"A disturbance of this magnitude is not apt to die in the public imagination soon," said Russo, adding that Senator Bergman "has given the pundits fodder for months."

Perhaps the most pithy condemnation of Bergman came from his friend Bob Dill, pastor of the Great Western Washington Church,

Bergman's congregation. "If the senator won't follow God, God won't follow him," Dill declared with crushing finality.

★   ★   ★

"Do you think Senator Bergman should resign?"

"Oh, hell yeah."

"Do you think Senator Bergman had sexual relations with an employee of Fantasies Incorporated?"

"I would have to say so, yes."

"Do you believe that Senator Bergman paid an employee of Fantasies Inc. to have sexual relations with him at the Seashell Hotel?"

"Is there really any doubt about that?"

"Do you think it is acceptable that Senator Bergman has yet to resign in the light of this ongoing scandal?"

"Totally unacceptable. He should have been fired a long time ago anyway."

"Do you believe Senator Bergman will resign within the next month?"

"He's never going to resign. Those Republican morons still love him. That's all he needs to keep going."

"Do you think it is acceptable for a United States senator to engage in sexual relations with a hired companion?"

"Maybe, but only if he's not married."

"Do you think Senator Bergman should resign if it can be proven that he engaged in sexual intercourse with a hired companion?"

"No."

"Are you serious?"

"Yes. Any other time, I would say he should resign, but with that arms bill coming up, I think he should stay in the Senate."

"So you support the arms bill—is that what you're saying?"

"Oh, God, yes. After what the Democrats did to the American military over the last eight years, we need that bill. We've become the pussies of the first world."

"So, if the senator were a Democrat, then you *would* say that he should resign for his presumed behavior?"

"If he was a Democrat, then I would say he should resign anyway, but yes."

"I see. So, can you explicate why you think a United States senator should resign for engaging in sexual relations outside of marriage?"

"Well, obviously, because people look up to their elected officials. It's up to them to set a Christian example for their citizens. If they fail in that duty, they devalue the entire office—and the citizen body with it."

"But you feel that the arms bill is a matter of greater significance?"

"In the short term, I would say so, yeah. I say we need that bill if we don't want Russia and China to be able to bomb the shit out of us with impunity. I'd say that takes precedence. After the bill is passed, well, then he might have to go."

"Then you think it is likely that the arms bill will pass?"

"Why wouldn't it? The Senate is split between the parties, but the vice president supports the bill. He'll break the tie—isn't that how it's set up?"

"And you think that Senator Bergman's resignation would compromise the chances of the arms bill passing."

"Hell yeah, these Washington liberals, they'll put another Democrat in the House as quick as blinking when Bergman goes."

"Which you're willing to accept, as long as it happens after the bill passes?"

"Actually, when you put it like that …"

Senator Bergman Released
from Custody
by Natalie Schroder
May 23, 20–

SEATTLE—Senator Milton Bergman, R-WA, has been released from police custody and will resume his ordinary routine next Monday, sources say.

"The senator is happy to be home and looks forward to getting back to work," says Gladys Martin, a spokeswoman for the senator's office.

"I'm just grateful to have my husband back," said Vanessa Bergman-Strauss, the senator's wife, who would not comment on the unfolding scandal emanating from her husband's arrest on suspicion of sexual relations with and violence against an escort.

Where Bergman-Strauss would not comment, the voting citizenry of Seattle has been less reticent.

"The senator obviously did it," said Dave Engstrom, thirty-nine, who nevertheless opined that the senator should not resign with the arms bill vote mere months in the offing.

★ ★ ★

"Hello?"

"Hey, Clarissa. How are you, sweetie?"

A pointed silence from the other end. The other end of the phone line, of the continent (Clarissa Bergman-Strauss attends one of the lesser schools in the eastern United States, not Ivy League, though of course nearly as expensive), of who knows how many spectrums.

"I know you're there, sweetie. I'm not going anywhere. How are you?"

A rasping breath whose hoarseness makes him vaguely wonder whether she has started smoking again. "I'm fine, Dad. I'm fine. How, er, how are you?"

"Oh, you know, same old, same old, ups and downs, no two days quite alike, you know how it goes."

"I certainly do. I guess."

"Oh, you're not going to be like this all night, are you? What have you heard?"

"What everybody else has heard."

"What has everybody else heard?"

"You're not going to make me say it out loud. It's disgusting."

"What's disgusting? I'm asking you what you've heard."

A sigh so exasperated as to recall one of her mother's. "All right, fine, if you're going to make me say it, it's been all over the news. They say you were arrested for beating up some hooker in a hotel room."

"I see. So, what's got you so upset?"

A hysterical whoop of laughter, sounding more like Vanessa than ever. "Oh, I don't know, my dad got arrested for beating up a hooker, and now his whole future—not to mention mine—is in jeopardy. Yeah, what's to be upset about? Yeah, I'll take 'Things to be Happy About' for five hundred, Alex!"

"You know, sweetie, sometimes you remind me an awful lot of your mother."

"Getting better and better, Pops. You always know what to say!"

"There you go again. That's exactly what your mother used to say when I accused her of sounding like her mother. Anyway, you don't actually believe what they say in those ridiculous tabloids, do you?"

"It's more than tabloids. It's CNN, KOMO 4—even Fox, for fuck's sake."

"Clarissa, sweetie, to quote the greatest president of the last five hundred years, that's all just fake news. Don't you know that by now?"

This time, when the snorts of laughter reverberate across the airwaves, he cannot help joining in, albeit faintly. Certainly he cannot keep a straight face.

"What actually happened then, Dad? Obviously, something must have happened. I mean, you *were* arrested."

"Do you really want to me to get into the details, Clarissa? You know I will, if you just keep pressing me for them."

She draws in another raspy breath without seeming to know what to do with it, and for the first time, a tremor of guilt floats across his chest. Somewhere over there in Virginia, perhaps in the same room as his daughter at this very minute, there is a girl named Miranda, also known as Clarissa's roommate, also known as Clarissa's lifelong best friend, also known as the daughter of the Bergman's next-door neighbors the Morrises of Morris Steel Imports, also known as the girl whose friendship with Clarissa was nearly shattered when, on Clarissa's sixteenth birthday, she walked into the private pool shower of her senator father's swimming compound to find her father and her best friend wrapped together, as they say, *in flagrante delicto.*

"Did you do what everybody thinks you did, Dad? That's all I want to know."

"Sweetie, no matter what anybody thinks, nothing anyone does is ever quite what anybody else thinks it is."

"Is there any chance that you will ever stop answering me like a politician?"

"Oh, Clarissa, I think we both know the answer to that question."

She laughs aloud this time, almost sincerely, and he laughs along.

"Either way, sweetie, you know that I have done far worse, and you still love me, right? Because I still love you."

"Of course I still love you."

"Well, that's good. And your mother loves you."

"Does my mother love you?"

That one catches him a tad off guard, but not too far off. "How the hell should I know? She loves yelling at me; that's for sure."

"Did she yell at you about, well, this thing, whatever happened?"

"Oh, no, she couldn't care less about what I get up to at nights. It's more what I don't do that gets on her nerves. That and everything else, you know."

"But I mean, seriously, Dad, do you think this is going to affect, you know, the big picture? I mean, everybody on the news, everybody keeps saying you should resign, that there's going to be a lot of pressure on you—"

"Clarissa, you know as well as I do that no force on this earth can turn a man away from the path that destiny has chosen for him, and my destiny is in Washington. You can be certain of that."

"Spoken like a true politician."

"I know you're being sarcastic. You sound exactly like your mother when you're sarcastic, by the way, but that's exactly what I mean. You remember that time—"

He is cut off by the sound of another voice, unintelligible but loudly warbling, on the other end, accompanied by the residue of a door swinging open, banging against a wooden cabinet. After some incomprehensible back and forth, he discerns Miranda's voice: "Is that your dad on the phone? Can I talk to him?"

His heart begins to race even as guilt floods him, thoroughly this time.

Clarissa sighs deeply and says with false brightness, tinged with real pain, "Hey, Dad, Miranda wants to talk to you. Should I hand the phone over to her?"

Under any other circumstance, he would probably have said yes, just to make his daughter uncomfortable. As it is, with all that is going on . . . "No, sweetie, but tell her hi for me, and have a good night. Love you baby."

★   ★   ★

"Natalie, I have an assignment for you."

"Let me guess."

"I want you to find the woman Senator Bergman was with in the hotel room that night. We need to get on top of this story."

"Why? Why do *we* need to get a jump on *this* story?"

It is a nice rainy Seattle day, yet the storm clouds outside are nothing compared to what is brewing within Karin's office.

"Oh, don't play naive with me, Natalie. No one else is going after the girl."

"I wonder why. A Fantasies Inc. employee? Who wouldn't want to follow that thread to its inevitable end in the labyrinth's maw."

"You're exaggerating, Natalie, and we both know it." Karin is an angular woman, midthirties, about ten years younger than Natalie, better looking than Natalie was even at the same age, and they both know it, despite their identical black pantsuits. They have worked together for eight years now and have never liked each other for some strange reason. "The first reporter to get a scoop on the girl—"

"You're just hoping Fantasies will pull a Ben Corker on me. That's what we both know for goddamn sure." Natalie has never been one to mince words. They do not go well with such high cheekbones, but Karin wouldn't deserve them anyway.

"You know I wouldn't wish what happened to that poor man on anybody, Natalie. I know you think I'm the Antichrist incarnate because of what I did to your friend Missy, but she had to go. As for this assignment, there is no danger involved. Corker got involved where he shouldn't have gotten involved. There's no convincing evidence that Fantasies Inc. actually did anything to him. It was his channels—"

"If he had been going after the governor like Cynthia Heiner did last year, would you say the evidence was unconvincing? You had no trouble believing that, as I recall."

"There was no evidence of back channels in Heiner's case—you know that. She was an honest, competent reporter who always did things by the book, and Governor Reich was always a violent, disreputable hypocrite with one leg planted on the wrong side of the tracks. He obviously ordered what happened to her. Ben Corker was another matter, and Fantasies Inc. is another matter. They are a powerful corporation, for sure, but they are not powerful enough—not *influential* enough—to have gotten away with what they have been accused of. And you are a much smarter investigator than Corker ever was. You're not going to get yourself involved with the wrong people. You have nothing to worry about. Just get in touch with the girl and get her side of the story. If you can't do that …"

"If I can't do that, then it will either be because somebody took me out and buried me in a bed of cement, or simply because of my own incompetence. In either case, you'll have no one to challenge your precious acolyte Marla when the time comes to distribute promotions."

Karin settles a leveled gaze on her and opens her mouth to fix Natalie in a formulated phrase. "This is an important story, and I am giving it to you, Natalie, because I have unending confidence in your abilities as a reporter and because this is the most important story going untapped in Seattle at the moment."

"Because no other rag has a reporter they so badly want out of the way—"

"Because this is a story that has the potential to impact every *woman* in this city, for that matter every woman in the state, every woman in the country."

Natalie is almost surprised when it does not escalate to the whole world.

"This is a story that emblematizes all the progress that has yet to be made for women in this country. It is a story that has the power to expose the depths to which masculinity and chauvinism are still embedded in the power structures of our entire society. This story needs to be told, and I am entrusting its telling to you."

"Why? Why are you entrusting it to *me?* Why would anyone entrust a story impacting *women* to me?"

"Oh, Natalie, despite everything, you *are* a woman. Or am I mistaken?"

"If you are a woman, then you might be. Just … clarify something for me. How *exactly* is this supposed to impact every woman in the country? Why is it so important to find the girl from the hotel?"

Karin fixes her with a steady, over-the-glasses gaze that could mean anything.

"Natalie, this scandal may already be the talk of the town, but as long as the focus is all on Bergman, we are only telling half the story. Worse, we are focusing all our attention on the man, on his side of the story. We need to get the woman's side. Do you think Bill Clinton would have sunk so fast if Lewinski hadn't spoken up? Clinton was so beloved that even her tragedy was barely enough to tarnish his reputation. If we don't get this girl's angle, Bergman will never face any consequences for his actions. The whiff of a scandal may be enough to make him wobble on his tightrope a bit, but without a real clincher, he'll never go down."

"So, is that what this is really all about? You have a grudge against Bergman?"

"I suppose you're a Bergman fan?"

"More than I'm a fan of you."

"Good answer. As for your question … well, I never would have voted for Bergman before this, but I did not despise him as I do now." She pronounces these words as flatly as the rest.

There is nothing Natalie hates more than obligatory contempt.

You could despise him for his politics. You could despise him because he's championing a bill that could indirectly kill fifty thousand children in a year. Instead, you make yourself hate him because of how he treats whores.

No doubt Karin feels a certain spiritual connection with such women.

On her way back to her cubicle, Natalie passed Marla O'Malley, Karin's personal assistant. In early twenties, Marla clutches a folder to her chest with her left hand and a steaming coffee mug in her right. She glances at Natalie through her winged spectacles as they draw near each other. "Good morning, Natalie!"

"Good morning, Marla." Drop dead, you ass-kissing bitch.

She is a curvaceous girl—that much cannot be denied. Not quite as pretty as she could be, despite her raven-black hair. Still less can be said of her personality.

"Karin keeping you busy?" Marla inquires chummily.

"Busier than you, I'm sure!" Heartily, humorously, to keep the sincerity of the statement concealed.

Natalie is squeezing her own comparatively scrawny ass back into her cubicle by the time she comes out of her reverie. At least she knows what she'll be thinking about when she picks up the vibrator tonight.

And now Karin the ice queen wants me to find the girl Senator Bergman was fucking and beating in a hotel. It might be possible to find out who the girl is. Fantasies Inc. is a powerful and secretive establishment, for sure, but they use the same computer systems as everyone else. Natalie knows a few people who could be helpful in that regard—if it comes down to that. And come down to that it very well might, considering how reluctant Fantasies Inc. has always been to let anyone in on anything related to their business.

Is it possible that Karin actually thinks Natalie can investigate them and pull it off? The slightest chance that she is not simply trying to get her in trouble, if not as badly inconvenienced as Ben Corker, at least to see her fail? Probably a mixture of both. Karin would certainly benefit from being the first to publish the story. Nobody else in Seattle has been stupid enough to go after Fantasies Inc. Not after what happened to Corker, not after what happened to Heiner.

But how bad can it be? Maybe Karin is right. Maybe Fantasies had nothing to do with what happened to Ben. He certainly did make some errors in judgment.

Going after one of Fantasies' leading attorneys, Malcolm Earhart, was a bad idea, for starters. Whether

Fantasies Inc. had links to the Mafia or not, Earhart obviously had powerful connections and few moral qualms in his conscience. It should have been obvious that he was not going to lie down and see his reputation destroyed by a cheap hack, certainly not without consequences.

And come to think of it, if Ben had been as smart as he thought, he might have known better than to implicate several other powerful figures in his investigation, publishing multiple pieces before the main investigation was even complete, indicating two other noted law firms with notable clients, a housing firm, a shipping firm, the Port of Seattle, all with possible links to Fantasies Inc., not only hiring them for their services, but also potentially using them to exchange money with the Mafia in exchange for cocaine and who knows what else.

Yes, the more Natalie thinks about it, the more Karin might have a point. Ben Corker may well have had primarily his own bad decisions to blame when a bag of PCP turned up among his possessions and he was taken into custody, tried, convicted, and sentenced to a lengthy prison term, a term that would have had a long time left—had Corker not died of pneumonia after less than two months after being incarcerated.

Yes, it could well be that Fantasies had nothing to do with what happened to Corker—or if they did, that they played only a grudging part, or only a minor part, probably not the *only* part, to say the very least.

Natalie is definitely a more intelligent journalist than Corker, and she is not going after anywhere near as dangerous a target. Karin just wants her to talk to the girl who was involved in the hotel scandal. Fantasies is obviously reluctant for that to happen, considering how thoroughly they have concealed the girl's identity up to now, but the girl cannot be too dangerous to them. What could she know? What angle of the story could be dangerous enough to put Natalie's investigation on par with Corker's?

Seemingly nothing, not at first glance, and yet a shadow falls across her brow at the thought, like a Seattle storm cloud, ready to lash her eyes with rain.

There is another more dangerous—aspect to this story. It involves a senator, a senator who is pivotal to certain ongoing national events, no less.

Yes, and Senator Bergman is by no means a less intimidating figure than former Governor Jules Reich. Less of a track record for duplicity, for intrigue, for suspicious coincidences often with a violent undertone, the whiff of a cover-up every other month, but still an independently wealthy man with powerful connections. And so was Reich—until an ambitious young reporter named Cynthia Heiner took it upon her platinum blonde, twenty-eight-year-old self to place the weight of an entire state upon her five-foot-three shoulders and figure out what had really happened that night when the governor emerged from a disreputable bar in SODO with blood trickling from his nostrils, no sign of a broken nose. Three days later, the bodies of two young Hispanic men—both of them with some interesting international connections—were discovered floating in the harbor. Evidence from the coroner's office suggested that they had been weighted down with rocks tied to their ankles. Perhaps the people who dumped them in the water were in a hurry and failed to tie them properly.

Anyway, the precocious Miss Heiner succeeded in bringing these and a host of other fascinating details before the eyes of the public, among them the fact that the governor had also been known to meet frequently off the charts with a man who called himself Jupiter Strong. Certain records and a noticeable facial resemblance suggested that the name on Mr. Strong's birth certificate may have been Martin Visconti, a close relative of Giulio Visconti, a known Mafia don who had been arrested six years earlier for gambling and trafficking in underage hookers, only to be released after less than a year in custody.

Had it not been for the fact that Governor Reich had already made himself despised by the state senate for his boorish behavior and constant reneging on private deals, the journalist's investigation might well have gone ignored at the highest levels. Sure, the governor might have been irked by the few protestors who showed up outside his house, but that comes with the territory of being a public figure, after all.

As it was, however, the Washington state senate decided to listen to the outcry of the public and brought impeachment charges against the governor, by now as unpopular among his fellow Democrats as he was among his Republican rivals. Despite the relative lack of provability of most of the evidence brought against him, the senate ended up voting unanimously to impeach him.

Governor Reich handled the news with his usual good grace, only using the words "faggots" and "pussies" twice apiece during the press conference at which he announced his impending resignation.

Two days later, Cynthia Heiner was found dead in her apartment. A bottle of pills suggested that she had deliberately overdosed on Tylenol. Less explicable were her motives and the large amount of semen discovered in her throat and stomach during the autopsy.

"She must have had a big gang bang with six or seven guys before she decided to kill herself," Governor Reich said when he was reached for comment.

A lone photograph sent anonymously to the late Heiner's boss suggested that the elusive Jupiter Strong had been in the neighborhood that same night.

Come to think of it, Natalie thinks, that name came up in one of Corker's articles as well—when he was ruminating on the Mafia figures potentially associated with the Port of Seattle and all the other institutions under investigation. They all tied back to an escort service known as Fantasies Inc.

And now Milton Bergman, Jules Reich's longtime friend and sometime political ally (despite their party differences), stands to lose it all, courtesy of his own connection with Fantasies Inc., even as the most important Senate vote of the decade looms.

If this does bring Bergman down, someone will call me some kind of a hero.

The thought, however, does not fill Natalie with the savage joy it should. Rather, with a nauseous trepidation, she gets a distinctive feeling that everything will not be all right.

CHAPTER TWO

"Everybody ready! All right, camera rolling, five, four, three ..." *Two one* mouthed silently, fingers descending, turning into an extended pointer finger symbolizing *go*.

"Good afternoon, everyone. I'm Kayla Roberts, here today with Senator Milton Bergman, the Washington state Republican junior senator, whose hotel room antics have recently become the talk of the nation. Senator Bergman, how do you feel you are being represented in the media with regard to this affair?"

"Since I haven't been watching the news lately, I can't rightly say I have a good idea how the media is representing me. That was a big part of what got me off the news in the first place. If they're not misrepresenting me, you can be sure they're misrepresenting somebody else. That's how it always is."

"Senator, with all due respect, you must nevertheless be aware that you are widely viewed as an adulterer who solicits escorts and then physically assaults them. These would be serious accusations even if they were *not* being leveled against a respected public figure, one who has spent the past twenty years advocating family values, proclaiming his Christian faith for the public to hear, and generally taking a socially as well as politically conservative stance in regard to all things sexual."

"I am aware of the accusations, and I am also aware that people will believe anything as long as it gives them somebody to sneer at. That is not how I choose to live my own life, and that choice is a direct reflection of precisely those values you have just named, which I have spent my political life advocating."

"In that case, Senator, you will forgive me for asking, bluntly, did you have sexual relations with that woman in the hotel? And did you physically assault her afterward? Perhaps more pertinently, if so, then why?"

"No, Kayla, I did not have sexual relations with the woman who was discovered in the hotel room with me when the cops burst through the door. And if we engaged in any form of violent contact, it was not initiated by myself."

"Senator, when the Seattle police entered the hotel room, you and the woman, generally believed to be an employee of the controversial 'companion agency' known as Fantasies Inc., were both fully nude. How do you explain that, if, as you claim, the two of you did not engage in sexual intercourse?"

"Kayla, my dear, have you never been naked in the same room with someone you were not having sex with?"

"No, Senator. I can't say that I have—and please don't deflect my question."

"Very well, since you ask so nicely, I will tell you what actually happened. You will be the first to hear the story, and so it is the version against which all subsequent tellings will be gauged, so please listen closely. I was up late in my hotel room dealing with calls, business as usual. I was at the hotel for a meeting with several campaign donors, by the way, a fact that can be verified. I decided to take a shower before going to bed, as I had not bathed all day, and it had been a long day. When I came out of the bathroom, the woman in question was lying naked in my bed."

"Senator, do you honestly expect me—or anyone else—to believe that?"

"Well, let me put it to you this way, Kayla. Do I strike you as someone who would be stupid enough to think he could get away with having a violent altercation with a woman of loose virtue in a jam-packed hotel in the middle of the night?"

"I don't really know you well enough to judge that, Senator, but it would not be the worst cognitive dissonance I've ever had to face."

"Be that as it may, Kayla, I can assure you, there is no reason to lend these accusations any more credibility than you are apparently willing to give my version of the story. My accusers claim that I brought this woman to my hotel room to have sex with her and then decided to beat her up for some reason. Why on earth would I do that? What conflict could possibly have arisen between us? I do not know much about Fantasies Inc., fortunately, but they do not strike me as an organization that would send out a girl with any great limits for me to transgress. Perhaps I did not have enough money to pay her what I had promised? But how could that possibly be the case, when financial concerns are one of the few I have never dealt with? Perhaps I was drunk. I admit there were some empty wine bottles in the room, made so by myself and by some friends, but I have never been a violent drinker. In fact, upon my arrest, I was breathalyzed, and my alcohol level was quite low. And there was not any other evidence of any sort of mind-altering substance uncovered in the room."

"Well, Senator, that is reassuring, but the question remains, do you expect me to believe that this woman just showed up in your room while you were showering? Then she took off her clothes and got in your bed for some reason?"

"Obviously, I have no control over what you believe—or what the public believes. In fact you, Kayla, have considerably more power over the public imagination than I do. Again, that's why I don't watch the news anymore. I live on the front lines, and that's where I prefer to get my information."

"Please just answer the question, Senator."

"Very well, Miss Fussy Pants. No, I don't expect you to believe my version of the story—no more than I expect anyone else to believe it. The truth is frequently difficult to believe. In any case, it is quite obvious that you have already made up your mind, along with most of the public. So, who cares? Nothing I could say would make any difference anyway, would it?"

"That is very true, Senator, but in my, and the public's, defense, it doesn't seem like there is much need for any difference to be made when the truth of the matter seems so blindingly apparent."

"Just as blindingly apparent as it seems to myself, and *I* was actually there."

"Senator, you say that you came out of the bathroom and the woman was lying there naked in your bed. What happened then?"

"Well, I can't say that I remember too clearly, like I say, I had had some wine, and it was the middle of the night, I'd been awake for probably twenty hours, so forgive me if the recollection is a little hazy. But as I recall, I saw her there, and I just about shit. *This is bad*, I thought. You know, in my mind's eye, I saw this whole thing playing out just about exactly as it has. I tried to handle the situation professionally, but I'll admit I was not in the best condition to do so. When she saw me, she said something like, 'Why don't you join me in the bed, Senator?' I asked her who the hell she was, and she kept pretending like I should know, like I had hired her. I hadn't, and I kept telling her so. At first, she tried to pretend like she thought I was playing around, and then she acted like I was crazy for not remembering her. Finally, she said that I must be crazy—and so she was going to scream for help. That was when I reached for my phone to call the police, to get this crazy bitch out of my room, and that was when she attacked me. She was screaming that it was in self-defense for anyone who was listening, but of course, in reality, it was to stop me from calling the cops and getting my word in first. And I'll tell you, she was a strong girl. I've never been much of an athlete myself, and of course, I was a bit drunk. Even more than that, I was exhausted, so the fight was just about an even contest."

"I see. And I assume this woman was commissioned to go to your hotel room in order to generate this whole scandal, that she was hired by political rivals, perhaps by your fellow Washington senator, Chloe Demetrio, all to smear your public image?"

"You know, I could have sworn she was muttering Demetrio's name while she was attacking me, but of course, it was hard to tell anything for sure."

"Well, Senator, that is quite the tale. If nothing else, I must admit that I admire it for its audacity. It takes courage to spew that much bullshit on live television."

"Oh, as a politician, that's nothing I'm not used to, Kayla. I'm sure you believe me when I say that, at least."

"Indeed I do, Senator. Indeed I do. I'm afraid we're already running out of time for this segment, so I'd like to get on to a couple of more pressing questions. While you have already stated that you have no intention of resigning as long as nothing can be proved, there is going to be enormous pressure on you to do so from a wide variety of sources. How do you intend to respond to your critics—beyond denying their claims?"

"As long as no one can prove me guilty, I have no intention of doing anything besides denying their false claims. But I will say this, personally, I do not think this level of vilification would be justified even if the accusations were true."

"It's interesting to hear you say that, Senator, because as a white male Republican politician, you have had to struggle against a bulwark of feminist opposition throughout your career, and now we have a situation where a strong undertone of chauvinism underlies the accusations against you. Are you saying that, if you had committed adultery with an escort, then engaged in a violent struggle with that escort, you would be justified in refusing to resign, that such behavior on the part of a United States senator would not be sufficient grounds for impeachment?"

"That's exactly what I am saying, Kayla. I have always believed that a politician's personal life and political life are two separate things—and they should be treated as such."

"Not to lay on the outrage too heavily, Senator, but you were already a member of the senate when, seven years ago, the female Democratic senator, Philomena Wren, was compelled to resign after having an extramarital affair with a male aide, compelled in large part by a wave of protest from her Republican male colleagues. Do you not feel that there is a certain double standard at work here?"

"First of all, Kayla, there have been no fewer angry voices raised against me than were raised against Senator Wren. Perhaps fewer of my fellow Republican male colleagues have spoken up to condemn me, so far, but on the other hand, I have already received far more condemnation from my female colleagues in both parties, all over the country, from female journalists, from feminists, and so on. Most of them spoke up on the other hand to defend Senator Wren seven years ago, so I see no reason why the double standard talk should be laid at my doorstep. Which brings me to my second point, which is that, as I'm sure you don't recall, I was among the few white male Republican politicians who openly spoke up to support Senator Wren at that particular juncture, and in that instance, I brought down the ire of Minority Whip Ken Poach on my head for doing so. I defended her on precisely the same grounds on which I have just defended myself: that a career in politics is like any other career. What matters in terms of one's eligibility should not be anything in one's personal life but simply, purely, one's capacity to do the job well. Whatever else I may have thought of Senator Wren's personal conduct, and of her politics for that matter, I respected and continue to respect her for her abilities, for her dedication to her country and to her constituents, for being a brave and intelligent woman in every respect. If it were up to me, she would still be sitting in a senate seat today. So, no, I do not feel that a double standard would be at work in my refusal to resign—even if there were a shred of truth to these obscene allegations."

The blonde woman in the gray pinstriped suit is silent for a moment. The camera unintentionally highlights the brief wrinkle between her eyebrows.

"Very well, Senator, I appreciate your candor. That was well put. One last thing before we finish up here. Assuming you weather this storm, do you think it will be possible for you to seek reelection during the next cycle?"

"If I can weather this, the next cycle will still be two years off, Kayla. People have short memories. I'm not too worried about it."

"For sure, although moralists tend to have rather longer memories, and one hears that certain among them have been feeling rather, shall we say, betrayed by this conduct on your part. Your own spiritual leader, Pastor Bob Dill of the Great Western Washington congregation, for one, who was most helpful to you in your last election."

This time, it is the senator's turn to hesitate. "You're not wrong, Kayla, and I'll admit that is a concern, even though Bob and others have been taken in by a false story. All I can say is that I intend to keep doing my job as well as I can, to keep my campaign promises, to protect my constituents' interests, and to conduct myself in as moral, decent, Christian a manner as possible. That's all I can do."

"Thank you for your time, Senator. I hope that works out for you."

They lean in to shake hands as the image on the screen cuts to the view of the camera farthest away, containing both of them in the picture.

The suit that Kayla is wearing is quite a modest one, but she has left the upper three buttons of the blouse unbuttoned, enough to allow him a glimpse of the top inch of her cleavage as she bends forward. Milton does not bother trying to conceal the glance he directs at it. If the cameras catch it, so much the better. *One more useless thing for the public to lose their useless minds over.*

He cannot tell if Kayla caught it or not. As they shake hands, as their faces draw to within two feet of each other, she mutters audibly, eyes fixed dead on his own, "You really are a disgusting piece of shit, you know that?"

But she probably would have said that anyway.

Bergman Accuses Demetrio
of Conspiracy in Scandal
by Natalie Schroder
May 26, 20—

SEATTLE—In a televised interview yesterday with Kayla Roberts of CNN, Senator Milton Bergman seemed to make what some are describing as an almost surreally absurd claim with regard to the ongoing scandal stemming from his hotel tumult last week.

"She was muttering Demetrio's name as she attacked me," Senator Bergman said in the interview, referring to the (presumed) Fantasies Inc. employee whom, he claimed, magically appeared unclothed in his hotel room while he was showering and proceeded to attempt to coerce him into sexual contact with her, finally attacking him physically when these efforts proved unsuccessful.

Kayla Roberts's subsequent skepticism accurately predicted the response of the majority of Washington voters to the claim.

"I can't believe that even Bergman can be such a blatant liar," said Sara Mallard, twenty-nine, who also described the senator as a "sexist" and a "hypocrite" and suggested that he should be convicted for his alleged misbehavior, a sentiment shared by 40 percent of voters according to a recent poll, 55 percent of them female.

Senator Chloe Demetrio, meanwhile, has fiercely denied Bergman's claims, accusing her Republican rival of attempting "to throw up a smoke screen more obscurant than anything Johnnie Cochran ever made up." (A reference to the infamously manipulative lawyering by the defense in the O. J. Simpson trial.)

"Senator Bergman is rapidly becoming the epitome of everything Senator Demetrio stands against," said Harold Bryce, a spokesman for Demetrio. "Being who he is and what he is, of course, he already represented a threat to

Washington's integrity as a bastion of left-wing progressivism and acceptance, but until now, he at least seemed like a personally sincere man dedicated to his conservative ideals. Now his image is crumbling, and all committed citizens should be quick to notice it."

They have indeed been quick to take note, but Senator Bergman is not without his defenders.

"I don't care what the senator gets up to in bed or anywhere else, so long as he keeps Washington from going from purple back to blue," stated Helen Pierce, forty-five, referring to fact that Bergman is the first Washington state Republican to be elected to the United States Senate in more than thirty years.

A key factor in Bergman's enduring support continues to be the looming specter of the much-debated arms bill, which seems to be serving to polarize bipartisan sentiments toward the senator, with Democrats increasingly shrill in their insistence that Bergman must go before September, while Republicans seem to have reached a silent resolution to maintain a death-grip on the 50/50 split in the Senate, safeguarded by the allegiance of Vice President Arthur Lime, who has vowed to break the likely tie in favor of the bill when it is put to the vote in September.

"If Bergman is ousted from office anytime between now and September, the arms bill is doomed," postulated Seattle University political science professor Deborah Kohl, who pointed out that, given the time frames involved, there would not be time to install a new senator in the position before the vote.

"Even if the Republicans won the position again, and that is highly unlikely, the House would still be split 50–49, giving the Democrats a guaranteed victory over the bill. But if they can keep Bergman in the House until then, it's another story altogether," Kohl continued.

This diagnosis has been questioned by some, among them Milo Reuters, an advocate for the Socialist Alternative in Seattle, who has suggested that some Republican senators might be moved to vote against the bill simply to spite Bergman if he is still a member of the Senate in September.

"If we look at the female Republicans in the House," Reuters said, referring to a body that currently numbers five senators, "and how they have been responding to Milton Bergman's behavior at the hotel, you'll see that they're speaking exactly the same way the female Democrats were speaking five years ago when President Sheridan's 'housewives' remark was all over the airwaves. He should've listened to them, but he didn't, and his banking bill got voted down by them for no reason except to make sure he didn't get away with his refusal to apologize."

Reuters concluded that the best chance for the Democratic opponents of the bill may be to keep Bergman in the House, going on to point out that, with him gone, the vote could still go against them in favor of the bill.

"The big news pundits keep simplifying the story, making it sound like the vote is bound to be split along party lines," Reuters claimed. "Actually, there is already evidence that some Democrats—some of the corporate-sellout Democrats—might be willing to vote for it. Certainly, it seems obvious at this point that the Democrats are not as united against it as the Republicans are united in favor of it."

If that is true, then Reuters may be correct to assert that the bill will stand a better chance of failure with Bergman still in the Senate to cause dissension in the Republican ranks and to galvanize opposition from Senate Democrats.

The overwhelming body of liberal opinion, however, seems to have settled conclusively on the necessity for Bergman's resignation, and some will be satisfied with nothing short of it.

"If Bergman is not prepared to resign, then we might just have to prepare him," was the ominous statement of Jana Stern, a spokeswoman for the radical group Lesbians with Guns, who added, "This arms bill has us up in arms, and we're going to leave a bill."

Darren Edgars is a tall fellow with a peppery beard and deliberately redneck clothes, a bit of a contrast with the rest of the clientele of the banal Starbucks where Natalie is meeting him, one of the countless venues emitting the composite smell of warmth and caffeine and cheap capitalism out onto the rain-soaked sidewalks.

If Natalie did not know better, she would take him for a contrarian striving to make a splash amid the streamlined grays and blacks of the conventional Seattle liberals. Instead, as she knows from past experience, the flannel shirt and cowboy boots are a ploy, one disguise among a repertoire, the products of a flamboyant personality with too much money and too few occasions for self-expression in this icebound city.

"Ms. Schroder," he says, smiling toothily from between his big Africa American lips, pushing back the chair across the two-person table with an elegant shove of his right cowhide boot. "It's a pleasure to see you again. Will you join me?"

She settles down opposite him with a mixture of amusement and apprehension. Although she initiated the meeting, he strikes her as the sort of man who always needs to be in control, to turn a situation to his advantage, for whom the original purpose is never enough, who would not have bothered to show up if he did not think there was the potential for more.

"It's good to see you too, Mr. Edgars," she says, removing her dripping wet overcoat and muffler, setting them down with her equally soaked purse on the already-wet floor beside the spindly chair. "Thank you for taking the time to see me again. You must be very busy."

"Must be? *Must* be very busy?" Bushy eyebrows at work in mock outrage.

"I'm sorry. Have I offended you somehow?" Her tone is mild, but she hopes the *somehow* adds a note of harshness. She does not have all day here.

"Oh, not particularly, my dear. I simply have this severe pet peeve for the assumption that there are forces in the world with the power to make me busy." He takes a sip of some filtered drink that even from across the table smells awful and grins at her again, but his ice-blue eyes give the lie to his jovial expression.

Natalie takes a sip of her latte and burns the tip of her tongue. "Well, be that as it may, Mr. Edgars, I *am* very busy, and as much as it peeves me, I would appreciate it if we could get right down to business."

"Business away, then, my sweet, business away," Darren says breathily, gesturing expansively with his hands before returning them to the table where, she notices, a newspaper is folded to reveal her latest piece on the Bergman scandal, the photograph of the senator smudged with spilled coffee, not an old stain. *Is this whole thing an artifice? If so, what kind of a ridiculous game is this guy playing?*

"When we first met, you told me that you had taken several photographs of Senator Bergman being escorted from the Seashell Hotel with your phone," Natalie pronounces, relying heavily on exaggerated lip movements to convey the words, reluctant to raise her voice even in this crowded atmosphere. "You also said that you had taken one clear picture of the woman who was in the room with the senator, although in the one picture you showed me, she was only visible in the background, quite blurry. Do you still have the good picture you spoke of?"

"As a matter of fact, I do," Darren says, almost too clearly, bobbing his head in affirmation, and then falling silent, much too quickly.

She is in no mood to play his games. *He just does this for the fun of it, doesn't he? He's not important enough to hold anyone over a barrel, but he wishes he was.*

They have been sitting in silence for nearly a full unblinking minute when Mr. Edgars finally blinks first. "So, do I take it you would like to see that picture?"

"As a matter of fact, I would."

"I see."

The silence extends much longer, and much more uncomfortably, this time. *What does he think I can offer him?*

"Will you show me the picture?"

"Well, that depends."

"Obviously. Because it *is* that big a deal."

"Well, evidently it's important to you. Perforce, it has the potential to be important to me."

"I don't suppose you would like to give it to me simply to be nice."

"I don't think so. You don't get to where I am by being too nice."

"I see, and where are you, exactly?"

"I'm at Starbucks with an attractive MILF who is asking me what I can offer her in exchange for what she wants."

They both know he has no interest in her as a MILF, which is precisely why she says, "So, what do you want? You want me to blow you for the picture, is that it?"

He purses his lips ever so slightly in genuine disgust before responding. "No, my classy dear. That's not quite what I was getting at, although I admire your dedication."

"Then what the hell do you want?"

"A little goddamn politeness would go a long way."

It is all she can do to keep from popping the filter off her latte and flinging it directly in his face.

Her teeth are still clenched when she pries open her lips to speak, but for the life of her, she cannot pry her jaws apart. The smell is getting to her, as it always does when she is so angry. Not the normal coffee shop smells, not even the aggravating tang of the rain on fabric and skin and polished surfaces, no, the smell of her own body, of her own sweat, the sweat that arises from the heat and humidity, but above all from the anger itself, choking her with its wicked tongue, exacerbating itself in a vicious circle, the snake devouring its own tail.

There is a look of faint surprise in Darren's eyes when he finally says, "That's all right, Miss Schroder. I'm sorry. You said you were very busy. I thought perhaps you were hyping it up so you wouldn't have to talk to me for long. My apologies. I see you are indeed under a lot of stress."

"Thank you for saying that." Her teeth are still clenched, but the stench of anger is slowly subsiding.

"You were asking what I want in exchange for the picture of the girl the senator may or may not have been violently fucking and tenderly beating that night at the hotel. Well, Miss Schroder, I am not an unreasonable man, nor is this an unreasonable demand, but we are after all playing with dicey stakes. The senator is a very powerful man, and this scandal has yet to be resolved."

I'm in an Italian opera. That must be it. I've died and been reborn as a character in an Italian opera. Hopefully I'll get to fall on a sword soon.

"Yes, Mr. Edgars, it is a high-stakes game, and yes, the senator might not be happy if he found out about your pictures. I don't intend to publish them—I promise."

His orchestrated features remain impassive, but his eyes are visibly relieved. "Thank you for that assurance, Miss Schroder. Now that we have gotten that out of the way, I can assure you that I do not want much for the photograph, nothing tangible at all in fact, simply a promise. Another promise, perhaps I should say, beyond your promise not to publish the photo with the name of the photographer, crowing it on a banner from the rooftops."

In spite of herself, her mouth twitches. "Okay. What other promise?"

"Simply a promise of gratitude, that I should be permitted to call upon you if at any moment in the future I should find myself in need of an investigative journalist to further my personal interests, on a one-time basis, of course, for a one-time service."

"That seems perfectly reasonable. You have a deal." The anger smell is coalescing into a migraine pressing at her right temple, but if it gets her out of there any sooner, so much the better.

He reaches into the breast pocket of his flannel shirt and pulls out a massive phone clad in a glittery powder blue case, bedecked with a shirtless Gucci model.

"Let's see. Let's see. There's Bowie, my beloved poodle. I have so many pictures of him on here that it's hard sometimes to find pictures of anything else. Oh, wait, here we go. Yes, nine days and thirty-eight pictures of Bowie later. Yes, here it is, the visual residue of that night at the hotel."

He turns it around to show her the screen. She snatches it away from him with a hurriedness that leaves him glaring at her reproachfully, but she doesn't care. She does not want anyone else getting a look at this. Perhaps he understands because it does not take him as long as she would have expected to stop seething.

He appears to have taken the photo precisely as the girl was being escorted from the hotel room by the police. She was not handcuffed, unlike the senator, not taken into custody, so all the sources claimed, and the picture bears that out. Clad in a white towel, she takes up most of the vertically inclined picture, flanked by the doorframe, still on the other side, the twin hints of the police officers on either side of her obscured by the doorframe and her dominating presence at the center. A tall, well-proportioned girl, midtwenties to look at her, sun-bronzed skin, curly brown hair, brilliantly wide brown eyes, muscular, all the benefits of the tropical sun rolled into one vibrant beauty.

Perhaps her pupils have contracted because Darren Edgars is regarding her now with the beginnings of a smirk, "Pretty girl, isn't she? I hear they really know how to put them together at Larsen's."

Natalie makes no reply but hastens to send the picture to her own Gmail account before handing the phone back to its owner.

He slides it back into his pocket and continues to stare at her, lips slightly parted, almost hungry looking. She carefully avoids his gaze, directing her eyes instead to her right, toward the long table in the middle of the shop, where a toddler in a blue coat has his arms wrapped around his mother's shin as she sips at a cappuccino and converses animatedly with another woman across the table, apparently quite unaware of her son wiping his snotty nose on her blue jeans.

Darren evidently has followed her gaze. "I would ask, but you don't strike me as a woman who has borne or raised children, Miss Schroder. Am I correct?"

The anger is getting ready to rise again. "No, I haven't. And yourself, well, I would ask, but you don't strike me as a father in any sense either."

He chuckles appreciatively, though his eyes have hardened. "You are quite correct, Miss Schroder. It seems you are every bit as perceptive as your articles have led me to believe. It is always quite satisfying to have one's suspicions confirmed, wouldn't you agree? Like a religious revelation, bringing solidity to the ephemeral."

She snorts aloud at that one. "Uh, yes, I guess I would agree with that, Mr. Edgars. Yes, it is, quite … satisfying, as you say."

This time she returns his steady gaze as he pauses before asking, "Have you ever had a religious experience, Miss Schroder?"

"Yes."

For the second time, he looks faintly surprised. "Yet I take it you are not a religious woman, am I wrong?"

"You are not wrong."

He nods, slowly, ruminatively, an expression of grudging respect making its way to his features. "Do you want to know what I think you are, Miss Schroder?"

"I have absolutely no desire to know *what* you think I am, Mr. Edgars."

He cackles uproariously. "I thought you were a woman who would say that!"

Still chortling, he wraps his raincoat about his shoulders and stands up, extending a hand to her across the table. She clasps it and rises as well, not yet moving to touch her personal effects, keen to let him get clear before she leaves.

She is ready to release his grasp, but he is not letting go. As her legs straighten, he leans in toward her and mutters, loud enough to be heard over the din of the room but only by her ears, "I think I know what you think I am, Miss Schroder. You think I am a queer little bedbug, a strutting peacock with a schizophrenic personality and an exhibitionistic inclination, a petty little man with too much money and not enough to do with it, a man who enjoys putting on masks for the sheer pleasure of confounding the viewer, a man who has worn so many masks his own features have worn away beneath them, leaving him with nothing but his masks."

What perverse twist in the cosmic design ever led me to cross paths with this freak? Why is it always the freaks that have the information you need? She lets slip no outward sign that he has articulated her thoughts exactly. His certainty is plainly such that confirmation would make no difference anyway.

He leans in even closer, his palm growing sweaty against her own—she can smell that same revolting tang of that caffeinated beverage on his breath—and he whispers huskily, "You are not wrong, Miss Schroder. You are not wrong at all."

Then in a whirl of leather, he is gone, disappeared so suddenly that her hand is still extended when she realizes that he has already vanished between the bodies crammed in the doorway, the coffee line that extends all the way from the counter to the sidewalk, shouldered his way between them without leaving any apparent indentation, no hint that he had ever been there, lost in the rain-soaked gray of the world outside, packed additionally with countless roving figures virtually identical, enough to render anyone anonymous.

She sits in silence for she knows not how long. In a moment of morbid curiosity, she picks up his discarded coffee cup, still half-full (or half-empty, she supposes) and peers at the label: *Grande Cinnamon Pumpkin Mocha Latte Combo.*

Apparently Mr. Edgars is even crazier than I thought.

She contemplates a sip, but thinks better of it and pours the remnants over the newspaper, her own article still staring up blankly from the tabletop.

That evening, sitting in the living room in her apartment, which she thinks of as her library, Natalie finds herself thinking unexpectedly of that anonymous photograph that linked someone named Jupiter Strong to the murder of Cynthia Heiner.

How many photographs can there be, how many videos, how many witnesses? Always enough to sketch the outline of a picture—but never enough to fill it in.

As she sets her wineglass down on the polished coffee table, her Siamese cat comes treading into the room. With a gentle mewl, Sapphire hops up on the couch beside her and purrs contentedly as she scratches him between the ears.

Her thoughts drift slowly back to the smirking Mr. Edgars, an anomaly if ever she met one. Too much money, too much personality, too much imagination, not enough time to spend it all. How can evolution account for such a creature?

And all of it a mask, to be taken off, to be replaced at will, by another, all for a price, of course, not an issue when you have that much money.

The thought clenches her stomach for reasons she does not want to acknowledge head-on. She gazes at the wall of books across the room, wondering how much money she has spent amassing the collection. Though many were gifts.

And to think how much bigger a portion of my income was consumed by those books, bigger by far than what Darren Edgars has spent on all his thousand-dollar suits.

At first, she thinks it is the inadvertent clench in her leg muscles that sends Sapphire bounding to the floor. Then she realizes that he is pursuing a spider across the hardwood, a damn big one, the sort that gives Natalie nightmares.

She has to fight down the gorge in her throat when the cat devours the arachnid, but she is thankful that it is dead. She mutters, "Good boy, good boy."

The cat returns to the couch, mewling in triumph.

That night, she dreams of a spiderweb, comprised of strands of shredded newspaper, fine print woven into delicately omnipresent strands, and at the heart of it all, the poisonous biter incarnate—with a pattern on its back that looks curiously like the face of Darren Edgars.

CHAPTER THREE

THE LIBRARY OF SENATOR Bergman's north Seattle mansion is his favorite room in the house. The dominating presence, even more than that of the books, is oak. The floor, where not strewn with the black fur of bearskin rugs, gleams with polished oak. The bookshelves likewise, and the wall paneling, the legs of the furniture that go all the way up and turn into leather, like the binding of so many of the books. That was one of his father's passions, binding his favorite books in leather, tracing the titles on the spines and covers in gold filigree. Milton Bergman does not share that passion, but he enjoys the contrast they present on his shelves, amid all the oaken ornamentation, the formal leather interspersed with ordinary hardcovers and the thick paperbacks whose spines have become wizened through so many openings and perusals. This is the room, more than any other in the house, where the senator finds solace.

Except, that is, when his wife is to be found here. Which unfortunately is most of the time now.

One consolation for Milton is that his townhouse in DC, the other big Washington in his life, also has a fine library. Not quite as oaken, not nearly as many books, but cozier, and, more importantly, entirely his own. Vanessa never joins him in the nation's capital anymore.

She is sitting there now in his preferred leather armchair, the built-in speakers gently blaring Mozart or Beethoven or one of those other German Romanticists. *At least it's not Wagner.*

Vanessa has always been a fleshy woman, prone to plumpness from the moment he met her. And to think, that used to be one of the things he liked about her.

Now her 250 pounds of nakedness is wrapped in her characteristic blue bathrobe, a color that likewise used to please him and now annoys him, albeit purely for its associations. Even more characteristically, she does not so much as look up when he enters the room, being far too wrapped up in some thousand-page paperback. He can tell simply from the thickness and the denseness of the script that it must be one of those French philosophies to which she is so partial— Deleuze, Guattari, Derrida—one of those Continental morons valued so highly for their rambling spewings.

Her gaze does not rise from the page, and it does not even stop tracing the lines as he begins to speak.

"Well, I'm going to church now." It is nearly five o'clock, Sunday evening, the hour of the big worship service at the Great Western Washington Church.

"That's brave of you."

"Oh, I don't know. The brave man is the one who fights even though he is afraid—or so I've heard. If there's one thing I'm not, it's afraid."

"That's brave of you."

"Yes, I suppose it is. The Reverend Bob is not happy with me, I hear."

"I wonder if he will make his displeasure evident from the pulpit."

"I'm sure he will. In fact, I'm quite looking forward to it."

"That's brave of you."

He sighs. Just sighs "I'll see you later. I guess."

"I wouldn't recommend it."

He is almost at the door when she says in the same flat tone, "Your mother called while you were out."

A few steps past the doorway, he comes to a halt and turns around. "Oh. What did she have to say?"

"Oh, nothing much. She wants you to go to confession."

His mother is a Quebec-born Catholic. She and his father never saw eye to eye on religion, nor he with them. His father was an equally ardent Lutheran. Personally, he would as soon forego attendance altogether, but his central body of voters do not care much for the *unchurched* as they call them. Bob Dill and his Seattle super-church came along at precisely the right moment, right before Milton was about to launch his first campaign for the Senate. A rabble-rouser with that supreme demagogic virtue, namely the ability to make the moderate seem extreme and the extreme moderate, ordinary, unremarkable, Pastor Bob has been most helpful in mobilizing every remotely spiritual element anywhere to the right of the political left in Milton's favor for fifteen years. By no means a fundamentalist, Dill possesses all the populist capacities, with the potential to appeal to every group on the sociopolitical spectrum.

The only problem is that he actually seems to believe in his ideals. Milton sighs again, much heavier than before. "I hope you told her that I would think about it."

"I told her nothing of the sort."

Is that a dark, sweaty tunnel constricting before what remains of his life, one way forward and no way out, and what remains only stickiness, hot and smothering, agony and regret at once, the pitiful molecules of existence rotting him away from within as dishearteningly fast and sickening as the constriction without, the tensing muscles between the thighs of the universe growing exponentially stronger even as his own grow weaker until (soon enough he knows) nothing will remain of him at all.

"My friends, I want to tell you a story."

The auditorium of the super-church is packed as ever. A crowd drawn from every corner of the city and its environs, of every age, every ethnicity, a few more women than men perhaps, but that is to be expected in any church nowadays.

Up on the wall behind the podium, behind the stage on which the podium stands, the projector blazes the stock image of the three utilitarian crosses perched on the hillside, shadowed, backed by the sunrise. The only thing that annoys Milton more than the anachronism of the image is the sheer kitsch.

Rather like his sentiments toward the man behind the podium. Anyone who looks at Pastor Bob can be under no misapprehension that they are looking at a man of God. Kindly, avuncular face gently lined by middle age, patience written into every plane, he always wears the same black suit jacket over blue jeans with a red tie to church, the same informal formality, as without, so within. There must be no doubt.

His voice, however, is a bit different tonight.

"My friends, I have never made a habit of attributing too much credence to the news media. They are, as we all know, an unreliable source of information. By far too much assuming, too much bias, too much corporate influence, too much — forgive me — too much *godlessness* have always served to distort the truth as it is presented by the professional news media. I prefer to find my truth in God."

A round of polite applause follows the pro forma statement. He does not wait for it to die down all the way, again unusual, before continuing.

"In recent days, however, there has been a story floating around the news outlets which I have found it impossible to ignore. A story which I initially attempted to ignore, because I could not believe that it could be true. I read this headline and I thought to myself, this is too much, the reporters have gone too far this time, this is absurd, this is unacceptable, this simply cannot be true. But then I saw another, and another, and I saw the photographs with my own eyes, and I could no longer deny it."

He pauses here for dramatic effect, glaring around at his spectators as though implicating every single person in the auditorium in his indictment.

"The photographs featured a face I knew, I face I have known for the better part of twenty years of my life, the face of a man I have admired, the face of a man I have respected, the face of a man I have defended, the face of a man for whom I have advocated."

The image of the three crosses disappears, fades into black, for one breathless moment the entire audience is convinced that Senator Bergman's face is about to blaze across the projected screen. Then it turns into a glorious picture of the sun rising between two clouds.

Pastor Bob seems unaware. Perhaps it was simply a coincidence.

"My friends, I am sure you all know the story to which I am referring. There is no need for me to denounce the person by name, which does not strike me as a Christian thing to do.

"I thought long and hard over how to capture my feelings toward this incident. Ordinarily, I would go with a Bible verse. But what verse could possibly express a situation so complex? What lone sentence could subsume the nuances, the pitfalls, the vortex of emotions?

"I ran it through every book in the Bible. I ran it all the way through from Genesis to Revelation. I ran it past every passage in the Gospels. In so doing, I came across many that came close, but none seemed quite to fit. Finally I hit upon the one that seemed least helpful, but most appropriate. It is the verse which, more than any other, has always, in my mind at least, captured the nature of the Christian's responsibility in regard to earthly power."

Dill pauses again, turning his head ponderously from side to side. The people at the back of the congregation, a hundred yards from the podium, can feel the anger throbbing from his gaze.

"'Give to Caesar what is Caesar's.' That, my friends, was the only verse I could think of that seemed appropriate.

"But what is Caesar's? Who is Caesar? Caesar was a dictator, a fascist, a tyrant, a king, an emperor, a despot. Caesar was everything that Jesus down came to this world in human form to oppose. When Jesus said to give the coin to Caesar that belongs to Caesar, he was not speaking merely of metal coins of cheap monetary value. He was talking about giving Caesar the entirety of his due.

"Ancient Judaea was not twenty-first century America. The Roman Empire was founded, in name, upon a democracy. Like us, they had a Senate with a hundred members. But they were governed by a despot, a man who was elected by that governing body to override their authority, because it was easier that way. They willingly gave their authority over to a dictator, because he relieved them of some trouble, some of the responsibility, some of the potential wrath of the people when things went wrong. In return, Caesar was given the power to do whatever he liked. He could sleep with whomever he liked, he could kill whomever he liked, he could behave exactly as he pleased.

"And because Caesar had absolute power over the state, the state was ultimately an emanation of Caesar. As Caesar came, saw, and conquered, so Rome came, saw, conquered. So they made slaves of the world. So they made sex slaves of the world. So they tyrannized the world, and the ultimate beneficiary was Caesar. Caesar in his palace, Caesar who was fawned upon, pampered, who bathed in gold and jewels, who could take a different slave into his bed every night.

"This is the man to whom Christ said we must give his due. What is due to a man such as this? What does such a man as this deserve?"

Another pause, another trembling hesitation. The auditorium is entirely silent, except for a few small children who do not entirely understand what is happening, why the atmosphere has turned so grim. Someone in the vicinity of Senator Bergman looks over and notices that the politician is hunched forward in his seat, his face amused.

"When Jesus was alive, the answer was simple: take up the sword and down with the tyrant. Contrary to what a lot of people seem to believe, Jesus was no pacifist. Why do you think Peter had a sword on his person when his Lord was being arrested in the garden? When Jesus rebuked him saying that he would die by the sword if he lived by it, he was not saying never to take up the sword. He was saying *don't be stupid with how you use your sword.* Regard the sword for what it is, a useful tool sometimes necessary to serve a purpose.

"Fortunately for us, we no longer live in a world where the only way to rid ourselves of a tyrant is to stab him twenty-three times. For the time being, at least, we still live in a country where we can speak up and hope to make a difference with our words. We can hope that we can change events with our votes, that we can persuade others with reasonable words and intelligent arguments to vote with us, and so make a difference in the world.

"However," and now his voice deepens, takes on an almost frightening texture, "as we all know, this does not always work out in practice. Because even now, more than two thousand years after Caesar was stabbed to death in the Senate house in Rome, still the Caesar of whom Jesus spoke is not yet dead. Still democracy is not always unimpeded. Still the system is polluted by demagogues.

"It is not without reason that pundits on both sides of the aisle frequently decry our democracy as an oligarchy, a system tilting ever more dangerously toward the sort of dictatorship that Caesar represented.

"My friends, I have spent my life battling against fanaticism of every kind. Fanatics of every sort strike me as a manifestation of Caesar. Fanatics among the religious of any denomination, Christian or otherwise, fanatics on the political left and on the political right, I abhor them all as antichrist.

"But what I despise more than any kind of fanatic is the fanatic who hides his extremism behind a facade of moderation. The man who is one thing and pretends to be another thing. The hypocrite. There is no worse kind of Caesar than the hypocrite.

"A hypocrite, in case you have forgotten, and it is a word which is used so often that it sometimes seems to lose all meaning, is someone who says one thing and does another. Why do people do this? Words are a powerful thing. A man who beats his wife in private and gives generously to charity in public will always be seen as a charitable man, so long as his wife-beating is not brought before the public eye.

"Hypocrisy, therefore, is a kind of tyranny."

Many among the congregation are nodding now, nodding that profound, thoughtful, religious nod. Senator Bergman is not nodding, but he is still smiling, the smile of one who is in on an inside joke.

"Hypocrisy is the most despicable kind of tyranny. What made Caesar a tyrant, above all, was not the people he killed, the nations he oppressed, the fact that he butchered Jesus on a cross. What made him a tyrant was that he could not even be honest about being a tyrant, he had to pretend that he behaved as he did for the benefit of the people.

"My friends, do you think, if the Roman people had known Jesus personally, and then seen him go up on that cross, do you think they would have continued to support Caesar? Do you think they would have given him the benefit of the doubt?

"I think not. I think they would have risen up like Simon Peter and struck the ear, not from Caesar's servant, but from Caesar himself. I think they would have torn down the Senate house upon his head and built a new one in its stead.

"My friends, we have before us such a conundrum now. Caesar is here, even now, haunting our nation.

"Again, my friends, I remind you, we still have the power of the vote. I thank God that I live in twenty-first century America, that I do not have to worry about taking up a literal sword in my bare hands to tear down the tyranny that is threatening to engulf it. But I have, if anything, an even more formidable task on my hands. I must do so by other means. I share this task with all of you, and implore you, like Simon of Cyrene, to take up this cross with me. It is a heavy burden, but if we bear it together, if we faithfully and sincerely implore others to join us, we can make it easier for each of us individually. That is what dedication, service, what the love of Jesus looks like. We must never forget the power of the vote. We must never forget the power of our Constitution, which invests us with the power to make demands, to demand the impeachment of Caesar when he shows his true colors, to compel him to change his ways if he can be compelled, to vote him out of office if he refuses. This is the power of the sword in our hands, and like Simon Peter, we must not love it for its own sake, but for the sake of righteousness, that by its power we may never fail to give to Caesar what is truly owed to Caesar."

Religious Leaders Take a Stand against Bergman
by Natalie Schroder
June 10, 20—

SEATTLE—In the midst of ongoing turmoil following the events at the Seashell Hotel two weeks ago, opposition to the embroiled Senator Milton Bergman has emerged from a wide variety of moralizing centers, most notably that familiar bastion of American ethics: organized religion.

For an elected official who has spent his public life advocating Christian, pro-family, pro-life, socially conservative values, this could spell trouble.

"As American Christians, we must give to Caesar what is Caesar's," proclaimed Pastor Bob Dill of the Great Western Washington super-church, Bergman's own home parish, in a sermon interpreted by many as a thinly veiled assault on his parishioner.

"Pastor Bob is not out to eject the senator or anybody else from office, but it is very important to him that Bergman, and the rest of his congregation, realize that the senator's behavior is unacceptable," said Gale Ross, a member of Dill's church staff.

Nor is Dill the only prominent Seattle religious figure to take a strong stance against the unrepentant senator.

"When the head is diseased, so is the body," said Luke Bouvier, the Roman Catholic archbishop of Seattle, who has already stirred political and religious controversy by speaking in praise of Bergman's rival, the Democratic senior senator, Chloe Demetrio, herself a devout Catholic who regularly attends mass at Saint James Cathedral despite certain doctrinal conflicts, most controversially her pro-choice leanings.

"If Bergman were prepared to repent for his actions, that would be one thing, for all men are fallible, but for a public official to so brazenly flaunt his sins without regret, that runs counter to everything we should be able to expect in the people we elect to lead us," Bouvier went on to say.

Conversely, the Episcopal bishop of Seattle, Jon Freeman, has been among the few to extend a degree of acceptance to Senator Bergman, stating, "To condemn a man for a sin he may or may not have committed without conclusive proof is not only unchristian, running directly counter to the principle of judge not lest ye be judged, but also to the legal principle of innocent until proven guilty."

Be that as it may, the court of public opinion seems to have settled irrevocably the matter of Bergman's guilt, not helped by the senator's own inability to contradict the accusations without lapsing into a laughably absurd account of events, and the chorus of moral outrage is extending well beyond the circle of conservative Christian voters on whom Bergman has long been dependent for his voter base.

"As a middle-of-the-road independent, I have always tried to avoid throwing my weight behind either party," said Rabbi Elias Ruben, president of the Seattle Jewish Fraternity, "but the leniency shown to Senator Bergman by his Republican colleagues and voters is enough to make me incline more than ever toward his liberal opponents."

Of course it goes without saying that the overwhelming body of Seattle feminist and atheist opinion has ridden against Bergman, having been among his most determined opponents since long before this scandal.

"This is just one more confirmation of what we have always taken that man (Senator Bergman) to be," stated Joyce Murray, thirty-eight, a spokeswoman for the Seattle Women's Atheist Organization, who briefly ran for office against Bergman in the last election.

★   ★   ★

"Yo, Natalie, you have a minute?"

"For you, Karin, I've got five … seconds."

With summer almost upon them, the sun is still shining outside at seven o'clock in the evening, hotter than ever, drifting in the general direction of the horizon, dyeing the no-longer-so-cool waters of the harbor gold, refracting off the windows of the cargo ships as they mosey across the surface with their infinitely patient determinedness. Across the radiant waters toward humid-hot Hawaii where only the most temperature-resistant organisms live anymore, toward ice-dried Alaska where fewer fish than ever float belly up in the radiation-poisoned waters.

"I just wanted to check up and see how you're getting along with that assignment I gave you, you know, last week."

Natalie rubs her fingers over her eyes, gouging the points of her middle fingers in especially tight, hoping Karin gets the message. "I've arranged a meeting with one of their local executives, a woman named Erin Hopkins. I'm supposed to meet her in her office in a couple of days, see what I can find out. I'm not sure how much she knows about me, if she's guessed what I'm after."

Karin nods, understandingly. *How unlike her. Maybe she has some ulterior motive. Actually, knowing her.*

"Well, whatever you do, be careful, Natalie. We have a reputation to protect here. You know that."

Better than you, you pontificating whore. "Of course, Karin, you know me."

"Yes, I do. Of course I do. By the way, I know I don't say this often, but you've been doing an excellent job these past couple weeks, keeping right on top of the Bergman story. I've been enjoying your take on the scandal."

The scandal you ordered me to drum up in the first place? Otherwise, how many people would actually care? And of course I've been doing a great job "these last couple weeks," you arrogant sack of … "Just doing my job. You know how much I love what I do."

"I know you do, and I admire you for it. You're one of those women who makes a mark wherever she goes."

Wherever I go. Because I'm going somewhere, is that it? "Well, it's always been important to me to amount to something. Which, like my father said, means make a lot of money. How d'you think *amount* got in there?"

Karin chuckles appreciatively and seems on the verge of responding when, with a rustle as disingenuous as herself, the fragrant Marla appears at her side, squeezing her substantial backside with some difficulty into the space between her boss and the other edge of Natalie's cubicle.

"Hey, Natalie! Well, Karin, I've got the office tidied up. You ready to go?"

"Just about, Marla, just about. Well, Natalie, I think that's everything. It's just about time for them to lock up the building. You almost done here?"

"Yes, I was just about to turn off my computer when you showed up."

"Ah, excellent. Well, you have a good night. Marla and I are just off to have a drink and then maybe catch the *Vagina Monologues* at the Paramount."

To which I am oh-so-pointedly not invited. Thank Christ. "Sounds like fun. You kids have a good time."

"Oh, we will. I'm sure."

"Good night, Natalie!"

"Good night, Marla!"

Cunt.

CHAPTER

FOUR

The morning of her meeting with Erin Hopkins, Natalie wakes up from a dream in which she seems to keep hearing the voice of a radio broadcaster announcing that the sun is never going to go down again. It will just stay up there forever, everything will go on as normal, and nobody will ever get too hot or anything. It will just be up there forever, like during that special season in Alaska, all over the world. Nothing to be afraid of, and yet, when she regains consciousness, Natalie feels like being sick.

Come to think of it, there was a moment near the end of the dream that may have catalyzed the nausea, when the stench of rotting fish seemed suddenly to arise from the residue of the thought of Alaska ... and then an unexpected intrusion, a closing shot, a flicker, like a pornographic frame inserted into the last reel of a big-budget family drama by a disgruntled projectionist, the hint of some sprawling thing, some convulsing mass, quivering flesh, no readily evident beginning or ending, stretched on the rack, rent at the seams, bursting with blood vessels and dead muscles, too hideous to be faced, censored at the last instant by waking—

She may have had too much wine last night. And earlier in the day. Sunday, her day off, is the day when she is most liable to be found drinking wine.

The volume may have increased substantially in the hours of the evening, when either her sensible side or her paranoid side urged her to do some more research on the organization known as Fantasies Inc., whose representative she would be meeting in less than twenty-four hours. That too may have been a mistake.

They are not an easy organization to get a grasp on. A sprawling corporation with branches in every state, and perhaps a few overseas, Fantasies grew up like a weed almost overnight, one stormy, tropically warm night about ten years ago. It was financed by sources not easily traced, defended by the best lawyers money—and maybe other motivators—can buy, and protected as such by ironclad user-agreement wordings that made prosecution for flesh trading virtually impossible. The corporation rapidly attracted a vast clientele that ranged across every level of society. In time, it began catering to the wealthy, the ones who could afford the most beautiful girls, the most convoluted fantasies, generating profits on an unprecedented scale.

With profits came expansion, from their initial nerve center in New York City to every corner of the nation. With geographical expansion came economic expansion, leading five years later to a much-publicized bilateral agreement with the equally meteoric plastic surgery (and so much more than plastic surgery) titan Ole Larsen. Fifteen years earlier, Ole had introduced the Unnoticeable Boob Job, a refinement allowing a woman to swell her bosom without any apparent incongruity, no incision scars, no inorganic solidity, nothing to indicate the artifice whatsoever except perhaps a disproportion in relation to the rest of her bodily features. That was the problem Larsen went after next. Right around the time Fantasies was being founded, he rolled out the Bodily Perfection Option, in which not only the breasts but any and all bodily features could be redefined to shape a person into a more perfect version of her/himself—all without any residual evidence of surgery whatsoever.

These twin pillars of the body trade were intimidating enough on their own before they joined forces. Now they represent one of the great partnerships of modern consumer capitalism. When Fantasies Inc. needs a certain type of girl, they send a willing recruit off to Larsen's, and Larsen's turns her into what Fantasies ordered, all for a very special discount. If need be, they can turn her back—or into anything else, whatever the circumstances require. So far, no ill effects have been detected after multiple surgeries—literally not a single one. Nor has Fantasies ever slipped up: not one prosecution, not one sexual harassment claim, nothing. Too good to be true.

It is enough to make Natalie's skin crawl.

Her skin does more than crawl. It breaks out in a cold sweat as she comes within sight of their Seattle headquarters, located among the newer developments along Queen Anne. Amid the shining glass and concrete facades, the glimmer of aluminum and steel all bedecked with posters advertising every manner of business, the sprawling complex of the Great Western Washington Church spread out across the slope not far behind it, the building rises proud and defiant on the corner of Queen Anne and Sixth Avenue, advantageously visible even from I-5, the banner at the top of the five-story structure proclaiming Fantasies Inc. in three-foot-high red letters on a bright yellow background.

The structure itself is an ultramodern affair, five stories of glass and steel rising sheer from the sidewalk, a hundred yards wide, probably the same deep, who knows how much basement and who knows what goes on down there.

The interior is paradoxically warm, more cozily proportioned. The foyer into which the front door leads is a circular space with white marble flooring, a relatively low ceiling with dim lighting, the walls black marble, interspersed with what appear to be portraits of important company figures. A few comfortable couches and chairs line the walls, low tables with magazines and lamps and ashtrays, all currently unoccupied. Two oaken doors face each other from the left- and right-most points of the circle. Twin elevators flank the receptionist's desk.

"Can I help you, miss?" The receptionist is a perky-looking young woman, brunette, bespectacled, the picture of a million receptionists the world over, for all the world oblivious to the Dionysian nature of the services that keep her fed.

Natalie wishes she could bite her. "I, uh, I have an appointment with Miss, er, Miss Hopkins."

"Oh, yes, you must be the journalist, Miss Schroder."

"Yes, I am."

"I love your articles. You're always so on the dot."

Natalie wonders who told her to say that. "Thank you. That's always better to hear than 'God, you're such a nasty bitch!'"

"People don't actually say that to you, do they?"

"More often in emails than in person, but you'd be surprised."

"I'm so sorry to hear that," the girl says distractedly, already fiddling with the landline on her desk, not sounding particularly sorry. "People always have so much trouble with a woman with strong opinions—yes, Miss Hopkins, she's here, the journalist, Natalie Schroder, yes. Yes … yes, I'll tell her, of course." The girl looks back up at Natalie without setting down the receiver. "Ms. Hopkins says she's very eager to speak to you—she wanted me to tell you that. If you'll get in the elevator to my left and press 5, you'll find her office at the very end of the corridor. It's very nice to meet you!"

"It's nice to meet you too, Miss?"

"Oh, just call me Cheryl!"

"Cheryl. Such a pretty name—for such a pretty girl!"

The girl blushes, but she does not seem to know what to say to that. She simply gestures toward the elevator and turns her attention back to her computer screen.

Subtle, Natalie, very subtle.

The corridor on which the elevator deposits her on the fifth floor is designed along the same lines as the foyer: white marble floor, black marble wall interspersed with oil portraits, oak doors leading into the offices of executives. The wall to her right, running along the entire east side of the building, along Sixth Avenue, is all glass. If the sun was out, it would no doubt be boiling.

Erin Hopkins's office lies, as promised, at the northeastern corner of the building, not to the left like the offices of the other executives but set into the very corner of the building, the black marble taking a sharp right and walling off the promenade.

Deep breaths feel childish at a moment like this. Natalie takes one anyway.

"Come in."

She did not even have time to knock.

Erin Hopkins is a, well, there is no denying it, a formidable woman. Tall without being gangly, broad without being broad-shouldered, curvy without being plump, all the right proportions in all the right places, so to speak. Natalie would be more impressed if she were not so sure that Larsen's can be thanked for the whole package, except maybe the height, but there is no escaping the overall effect. A tingling near her groin tells her that, if she were a man, she might already have a hard-on.

"Ms. Schroder, I am so pleased to meet you!" Extending a muscular but pleasantly soft hand, she clasps Natalie's own firmly and directs her to the chair across her desk, all in one expansive movement.

Settling behind her substantial backside in the leather chair behind her desk as the journalist takes the seat proffered, Miss Hopkins smiles broadly, resting her hands behind her head and leaning back casually in her swivel chair, staring into Natalie's eyes with an unblinking gaze that would be piercing if it were not so genial.

The sort of geniality disguises the taste of poison. "Thank you for taking the time to meet with me, Miss Hopkins," Natalie begins, wishing she did not sound like she were trying to sound like her usual acerbic self. "I'm sure you have a lot on your plate."

"Not as much as you might think," the fleshy woman replies, leaning forward now, causing Natalie to notice her clothes for the first time, the black V-neck blouse that peeks out from between the lapels of her dark blue suit jacket, offering a generous view of her endowments. The tingling increases. "Once you reach a certain level, it's mostly just taking calls, yelling at people, drinking before noon. That's off the record, of course."

"Obviously, I wouldn't dream."

"Well, Miss Schroder, or would you prefer I call you Natalie? I certainly don't mind if you want to call me Erin."

"That's very kind of you. Yes, first names is fine."

"Excellent. Well, Natalie, let's get right to the point. In light of what's going on in the world right now and in light of what you have been writing about for the last two weeks, I'm assuming you are here in connection with poor Senator Bergman's recent troubles, in relation to an employee of mine."

"That's quite astute of you. Yes, Erin. Indeed."

"Well, Natalie, I am sure it goes without saying that this organization relies on the utmost confidentiality in every aspect of its dealings."

"That's why you have a headquarters that can be seen from the other side of Seattle, I take it."

"The best secrets are hidden in plain sight. The lies that politicians spout on live television, the lies that witnesses tell on the stand, the lies that journalists put into print, the bolder the lie, the more likely people will believe it. You know this."

"Yes, I suppose I do."

"So, you understand what I am getting at when I say that I cannot possibly just let you talk to the unfortunate girl who found herself in so much trouble with one of our most respected and dedicated clients."

"I had a feeling that would be your approach. But you must have had some reason for allowing me to come here, for putting on all this production, if you don't mind me saying so, Erin. So, what *are* you able to tell me? Aside from the interesting fact that Senator Bergman is a devoted client of yours?"

"Frankly, nothing at all, my dear, and if I thought that you could do anything with that information, if I thought that it did not go without saying that I am not going to allow you to quote me under any circumstances, I would not have said that much."

"I see. Then why did you agree to meet me at all?"

"I wanted to meet you. I've been following your articles for a while. You are an interesting woman. It pays to have friends among the media. And you strike me as a woman who could be a very valuable friend under the right circumstances. Propaganda is the most powerful tool in the populist arsenal."

Is that the fingers of Doom, inching their way toward my neck? "Well, Erin, I appreciate that, but with all due respect, I believe very strongly in an informed, unbiased electorate, as opposed to an informational dictatorship. The world saw enough of that with Goebbels. As well as an investigator of the present, I am a student of history."

Erin puts on a good show of looking mildly abashed. "I hope you don't think I was trying to recruit you away from your calling, Natalie. Oh my goodness, no. To use your phrase, with all due respect, I'm not certain if it is possible to excise bias from the human experience—in a way, I think democracy depends on it—but I take your point. No, all I meant was there is a time to every purpose under heaven. We all have moments when we find ourselves reliant on others for our own benefit, if you know what I mean."

"I … I'm honestly not sure that I do, if you'll forgive my denseness."

"Well, what I mean is, Natalie, you have a powerful voice, and it comes across in what you write. That's why you have so many readers, so many fans, and, I believe, a few enemies. Fantasies Inc. knows a thing or two about that."

"I believe you."

"Everyone needs friends sometimes, but controversial people, controversial organizations, they need friends more frequently than other people, precisely because they make enemies more easily."

"I suppose you have a point there."

"So, when I say that it pays to have friends among the media, I mean that it is paramount for a controversial organization like Fantasies Inc., precisely because we have so many enemies and potential enemies among the public at large. A widely read journalist such as yourself has the potential to wield a great deal of influence over the perceptions of the public. I would, of course, never ask you to compromise your journalistic integrity by printing anything that was untrue or by obscuring or omitting anything that you felt the public should know. What I mean, rather, is that, since all human beings have their own point of view, and bias, far from being an enemy of individuality, is in fact the essence of the individual point of view, the personal views of a journalist are inevitably a part of what they publish.

For instance, if a journalist is a liberal, and he is writing about a political subject, you would not condemn him if you uncovered a trace of a liberal bias in his article, would you? You would not call that a distortion of the truth, of his integrity. You would simply say that he is doing his job, portraying the facts as he sees them. If his perception is defined in part by his biases, well, that is simply in the nature of perceptions. You follow?"

"Er … I guess I do."

"So, when I say that I would like for us, you and I, Fantasies Inc. and the influential journalist Natalie Schroder to be friends, I mean only to say that such a friendship might incline some of your articles every so faintly in our favor, if such an occasion should ever arise when we should cross paths again. In much the same way that a liberal political correspondent might incline to present a negative view of Senator Bergman even in an ostensibly objective article, where a conservative journalist might be more forgiving of the senator's transgressions. Does that strike you as a reasonable request, not unduly burdening your fact-peddling conscience?"

Is that hint of contempt I am detecting, or am I just being sensitive? "I … I would say that is a perfectly reasonable request, Erin, if your own friendship is sincere."

Erin laughs, that sort of laugh where the head is tilted up, the mouth opened deliberately wide, a cackle conscious of itself. "Oh my dear, Natalie. Are you suspicious of me? Do you have trouble trusting the word of a flesh-trading corporation on its face?" She laughs again, and Natalie joins her, just to be a sport. "I'm just kidding, of course. Come to think of it, I don't think I actually got around to offering you anything in exchange for your friendship."

"No, come to think of it, you didn't."

"Well, Natalie, Fantasies Inc. is a very professional establishment, and as I'm sure you know, we cater mainly to the desires of the advantaged. Although we retain our less expensive options, they are not our main moneymaker anymore. We turn a profit by providing wealthy men and sometimes wealthy women with companions specifically designed to please them, by arranging specific scenarios. It's all in the specifics; the specifics are what sell."

"That makes sense. That's capitalism in a nutshell."

"Indeed it is. But, as any good student of economics knows, sometimes a business has to make certain sacrifices in order to make a bigger profit in the long run. Sometimes one has to be generous if there is to be any hope of receiving generosity in return. The logic behind sales, discounts, buy one get one free, et cetera."

"Oh, is that why they do that? I thought they were just being dumb."

That laugh again. "In that case, let me convince you. Allow me to give you a hands-on demonstration of the power of generosity. I would like to offer you, Natalie, a temporary, free membership with Fantasies Inc."

Her heart trembles faintly, she is embarrassed to notice. "I, um, okay."

"Ordinarily, it is five hundred dollars for a membership, and depending on the fantasy requested, aside from the most basic services, a thousand dollars per meeting, plus whatever is required to fulfill all the specifics. It usually ranges up to at least five thousand, frequently much more than that."

Natalie whistles. "I'm beginning to understand the size of this facility."

"Quite. But since we are friends now, Natalie, I want you to enjoy some of what we have to offer for free. No offense, but I'm sure a journalist's salary is not enough to afford most of what I have just mentioned."

A snort rises in her throat that she suppresses only with difficulty. "That's, uh, that's one way to put it, yes, Erin."

"Therefore, I propose to give you a one time free trial, to be used whenever you wish. I have a form for you to fill out. Here's a pen. If you would like to do this right now, we can save ourselves a great deal of trouble later. I'll take it when you're done, and whenever you want to cash in the deal, you just call the number on this card, you see? All right, there you go."

Natalie glances over the document. Only a few pages in length, but filled with some penetrating questions, no pun intended. *Describe, in three sentences, your ideal sexual encounter. Describe, in three sentences, your ideal sexual companion. Where would you wish to meet your ideal sexual companion? Describe, in one word, your dominant personal fetish.*

The pen scratches over the surface of the paper with what feels an almost comical officiousness. Erin never seems to lift her eyes from Natalie's face, nor does she ever seem to blink. The sheer challenge behind that gaze is the only thing that makes the embarrassment endurable.

When Natalie hands the document back to her, Erin takes it without a word and stands up, turns around, and deposits it in a filing cabinet behind her desk, bending over to do so. She is wearing a form-fitting black skirt, much like those favored by Marla, and as with Marla, it is quite a form to fit. The only difference is that, whereas Marla's skirts typically reach down at least to the knee, Erin's skirt barely reaches beneath her buttocks—when she is standing straight.

She does not appear to be wearing anything under the skirt.

Natalie is already on her feet, collecting her bag, by the time Erin has straightened up, turned back to face her.

"Going already? Well, it has been a pleasure meeting you, Natalie, a real pleasure. And I think a profitable meeting for us both!"

"I … certainly hope so, Miss, er, Erin. I certainly hope so."

She has extended her hand, but Erin does not seem keen to take it. Instead, the tall woman, she is at least two inches taller than Natalie, strides purposefully around the desk and boldly wraps her strong arms around her.

"How do you feel?" Erin breathes huskily in her ear.

"How do you think I feel?" Natalie does not care for the tone of the question.

The woman cackles again, more sharp-edged than ever. "You felt what I allowed you to feel. That is the way it works here, Natalie. I hope you are prepared for what we are offering you." She cocks her head at a jaunty angle, contempt dripping silently from every facet of her face. "Now, if you don't mind, Miss Schroder, I have another meeting in a few minutes. If you would please show yourself out."

On the way back down the hallway, her attention perhaps heightened by the blood pounding more noisily than usual through her veins, a certain absence registers itself at the edge of Natalie's vision. Perhaps on any other occasion, she would think nothing of it. Perhaps it was there before, and she missed it in her initial nervousness. Or perhaps it juts out because it is a discrepancy, an alteration. She will never remember for sure—that's the hell of it.

She has already walked past it when she comes to a halt, forces herself to turn around, knowing that she will not be able to shake the feeling.

The oaken executive doors all have the names of their occupants inscribed in them on plates, small metal placards fitted into the prescribed slots at eye level. All the way up and down the hall, more than a dozen of them, the doors interspersed by the oil paintings, probably not paintings of the rooms' occupants, though who knows.

One of the doors is missing a placard. There is no name there, only a blank rectangle of oak between the two metal slots, black lines on a flat brown surface.

Two men in suits stare down at her from either side of the door. One of them looks vaguely familiar, though so does the other, in a way, both weathered African American faces, condescending, unconcerned.

The door shows a sign or two of having been used recently. Traces of grease on the handle, a certain personality in the appearance of the wood, the light under the door, nothing to suggest that the office is not in use, save that absent placard.

Even if Karin wasn't trying to kill me, I think she's going to get her wish.

Heading back into the heart of Seattle, Natalie turns up the volume on her car radio louder than usual, then much louder, in an effort to drown out the echo of Erin Hopkins' voice. It does not begin to work until the familiar nasality of local newscaster Connie Rothes intones: "Violence erupted today on the site of the killing of Arnie Oldman by the so-called SODO 3, where a group of racial justice activists had gathered to commemorate the police brutality victim. The proceedings were interrupted by white supremacist counterprotesters allegedly headed by several masked police officers, though this claim has not been confirmed."

A hot stab of anger clenches in Natalie's stomach, pulverizing the more ephemeral disgust induced by Fantasies Inc. It's probably for the best that Karin assigned the SODO 3 to one of her other protégés. Natalie struggles to contain the strength of her emotions when she writes about subjects she doesn't care about— Senator Bergman's hotel foibles, for instance. The SODO 3 might cause her entire column to burst into hellfire.

★   ★   ★

"Hello?"

"Hi, Bob."

"Hello, Senator." The frost in Bob Dill's eyes is palpable through the airwaves.

"How's it going, my old friend?"

The coldness deepens, hardens, with it Bob's voice.

"Depends what you mean by *it*, Senator, depends a great deal."

"Now, Bob, if you're mad at me, why don't you just spit it out? Men like you and me, we don't have to beat around the bush."

"I didn't realize I was beating around the bush, Senator. I thought I was struggling mightily to be polite, despite a powerful temptation to be otherwise. Some of us, you see, are still capable of resisting when the devil comes a-knocking."

"Now, Bob, as you yourself have said so many times, all men are sinners."

"Indeed they are, but some are more sinful than others. Not that one expects a politician to be any less a sinner than anyone else, but there are limits."

"Of course there are limits, but why does the limit always get drawn right next to the sex mile sign? What is it that is so much worse about enjoying a girl's body compared to ordering a missile strike on a third world country?"

"Tell you the truth, Senator, I could have lived with the solicitation, even the violence, if you hadn't felt the need to lie about it, and so ridiculously at that."

"Well, what was I supposed to do, Bob? Stand up there in front of a million voters and say, 'Hi, folks. I regularly cheat on my wife because it was a marriage of convenience to begin with, and I wouldn't be attracted to her anymore anyway?'"

"Is that true, Senator?" If it was the depths of winter before, it's getting toward the North Pole now. Not that the North Pole is as frozen as it used to be.

"Yes, Bob. As a matter of fact, it is true. Vanessa's a lesbian, did you know that?"

"From some of the things I've heard you say about her, I suspected, but that still does not make it morally permissible for you to commit adultery—or to lie about it. That's two of the Ten Commandments right there, among other things."

"So, what should I do instead? Stay faithful to my lesbian wife forever?"

"You should never have married her if you knew she was a lesbian, no matter what the advantages were. Since you did, yes, so long as you are married, yes."

"Well, I gotta hand it to you, Bob. You are consistent, if nothing else. That's such a rarity in the righteous these days. Probably always was, I suppose."

"Quite the contrary, I am as much a walking contradiction as you are, Senator. I'm just less of a *hypocrite* about it." The way he says the word, Milton can see the spittle flying from his lips.

"We're all hypocrites, Bob. That's the point of contradictions. If you're as contradictory as I am, then you're a hypocrite. If anything, you're more of a hypocrite for claiming that you aren't."

"I'm honest about my contradictions, my shortcomings. That's not hypocrisy. That's self-awareness. That's striving to be better."

"How much better if you don't try to change yourself—if instead you wear those flaws like a badge of honor? Seems like that's more how you pastors and evangelizers are always treating them. Makes hypocrite seem apt, whatever you say."

"A lot of preachers do that. I don't deny it. Perhaps I do too—to some extent. But don't say that I don't strive to better myself, Senator. I could be a millionaire with a congregation that size. I chose not to be because that is not what being a pastor is supposed to be about. There was a time when I might not have made that decision. When I started out, I admit, I enjoyed some of the advantages that my position brought me. That changed when I went to Africa. I started to understand the true meaning of the parable of the woman who gave her last two coins to the temple."

"That's a truly touching story, Bob, but in all honesty, that still kinda sounds like a marketing strategy. You still have a lot bigger income than any starving child in Africa. And most of the ones getting your money are still starving."

"Be that as it may, they would be hungrier without me, and I would be richer without them. We can only do so much in this world, Senator."

"That's exactly right. We can only do so much because we are only human. That's why we have to forgive others for their human failings, right?"

"That depends."

"That *depends*?"

"Jesus may forgive everything, but it is up to him. It is not for me to pretend to know his mind. Men can only forgive what seems forgivable. Part of being human."

"Well, isn't that just the most convenient loophole I ever did hear of, Bob. You got any more tucked away up your sleeve? Might come in handy someday."

"Are you about finished, Senator? What are you really after?" At least his voice is not so icy now, more haggard, exhausted. What Milton has been waiting for.

"All right, since you ask it like that, I'll put it simply, Bob. I want you to stop attacking me—from the pulpit and in the press. That's all I'm after."

"Why would I do that? Simply asking does not earn you a reprieve."

"Very well. What *would* earn me a reprieve?"

"First of all, whatever it was, you would have to be sincere, not merely doing it to make yourself look better in the public sphere. Does that seem plausible?"

"I think we both know the answer to that one, Bob."

"I think so too, and that's why I'm not going to bother. I have always believed in second chances, but if life has taught me anything, it's that once a person lets you down as thoroughly as you have let me down, they never redeem themselves. Even if they worm their way back in, they always let you down again. Just how it is. As far as I can tell, that's how God made the world. Not the most upsetting thing about his creation, all things considered."

"Let me ask you one more thing, Bob, if you don't mind. You've supported me all these years, you've said, because you believed in my vision, because you thought my ideas were more Christian than Demetrio's and the others. And, of course, because you thought I was a better personal example than them. I can understand how you might have changed your mind on that last one. But what about the rest? Is that more important than the rest? Are you willing to see a Democrat in my seat? You want to see abortion on demand again, taxes through the roof, Caesar taking way more than his due? Is what I do in my own bedroom a bigger deal than all that?"

A dry chuckle reverberates across the waves, more sad than disgusted.

"Senator, I couldn't care less what you do in the bedroom. I don't care that you cheat on your wife, that you lie in public, even that you lie about lying in public. What I care about is basic human decency. I would rather see a politician do the wrong thing for the right reasons than the right thing for the wrong reasons. The reasons are what ultimately matter because our reasons are who we really are."

"I'm pretty sure nobody's reasons are perfect, Bob."

"I'm sure they're not, but we do our best. That's all we can do."

"Well, thank you for your time, Bob. You're a good man—whatever else I may think of you."

"Thank you for saying that, Senator. And I know you're doing the best with what God gave you. Apparently not as much as I once hoped."

When the line has gone dead, Milton Bergman sits a while longer with his phone still pressed to his head. The screen on his laptop is the only source of light in his study, a smaller version of the library, more compact, almost as many books in it but less than half the space. The image is blinding against the pervasive night, but if Milton only ever sees one image again, he would just as soon it be this one.

A tall man with a bald head that contrasts with his neat, inch-long beard is waiting outside the study when Milton steps out into the hallway at last.

"Was Pastor Bob helpful in any way, sir?"

"I'm afraid not, Terrence. I'm afraid not. It looks like we're going to have to take drastic measures. Messy, very messy."

"How unfortunate. Pastor Bob seems such a nice man."

"He is—a Reformer of the purest pedigree—brave, sturdy, dependable, learned, wise, incorruptible. The pitiable fool."

"Do you want me to get on it right away, sir?"

"I think not. No, this is going to require great precision. Dealing with the public is like performing surgery—so many potential complications. You must take your time, explain each step of it as you go along, for yourself as much as for the patient. The one good thing about scandals is that they grow boring quickly. Once the initial shock wears off, the details become banal, predictable, familiar from countless iterations. Even the pleasure of moral outrage grows stale before too long. The people need to be ready. They need to have lost their taste for the appetizer before we lay another plate in front of them. Much tastier that way—and it drives away the memory of what came before."

"As you say, sir. I know you are a master surgeon."

"I'm a rank amateur, Terrence. The trick in politics, as in any other field, surgery especially, is to *look* like you know what you're doing. Appearance is everything."

For instance, if you appear to be living, that's all you need to keep them from guessing you are dying.

CHAPTER

FIVE

Alan's apartment building is in the most clogged artery of the heart of Seattle: the downtown cavalcade where the old brick rectangles huddle amid the glassy high-rises like fearful children beneath their glittering adolescent siblings.

Alan, predictably, makes his squalid living in one of the lesser squatting places, one of those structures where the bottom level is comprised entirely of shopfronts, pinned down by what looks like an unbearable weight of brick, faded remnants of red and brown, spotted here and there with desultory flowerpots in the blank windows.

Natalie sits in her Honda, waiting for Alan to text her and growing squirmier by the minute. There is nothing she hates more than waiting.

The heat of summer has reached Seattle at last, nearly halfway through June, still without the clear

skies and brilliant sunlight. The gray sky exacerbates
the mugginess, making it a pain to breathe anywhere.

Is this how johns feel, waiting for their mistresses?

"Cum on up nat." Such is his message to her. Helps
her remember where she ranks in the scheme of things,
if nothing else, if truly nothing else.

The elevator has an out of order sign swinging from
its antiquated face. She will have to climb sixteen floors
under her own steam.

The coming down, at least, should be easier. If all
else fails, she can simplify things and take a nosedive
out a neighboring window. She has contemplated it
before, visiting Alan, even when the elevator was in
working order.

Natalie does not bother knocking when she comes
to his lonely door. She knows he will have left it
unlocked for her. Whenever she has knocked in the
past, she has been commanded imperiously to come
in. Courtesy is wasted on cretinous Alan in any case.

"You ever heard of knocking?"

"No. What's knocking?"

"That's okay. I'm just funning you."

Alan is what might be described as a heavyset nerd,
late twenties, with no beard on his babyish face and
no sense that he is in the habit of taking a razor to it.
Spiky black hair the same color as the T-shirt he wears
over his gray boxers, which along with a white sock
emblazoned with a red–yellow–blue target on the heel
are his only raiment.

The apartment itself cannot be described in any reliable terms, for it is nearly impossible to make out the actual topography. Alan is not a hoarder; he is simply disorganized. In the extreme.

The thick white carpet (here and there, an inch or two of it can be glimpsed for what it is) groans under the weight of a veritable mountain of gadgetry, books, DVD cases, CD cases, pornographic magazines, and a wide variety of other magazines (although the pornographic ones are by far the most in evidence, along with some of the DVD cases), bags of chips in varying degrees of emptiness, some of them still unopened with sell-by dates two months out of date.

Alan is sitting on what appears to be a black leather couch, cross-legged with a disproportionately massive laptop on top of his lap, somehow failing to conceal the hole in his underwear from which an entire testicle protrudes, as hairless as his chin and cheeks. "What took you so long anyway?"

"I had to climb up sixteen flights of stairs. Your elevator's broken."

"Oh, Christ. I forgot to take down the signs, didn't I? I put those up as a joke. The elevator's fine."

The glare she pours into his childlike face goes quite unnoticed.

"Anyway, if you'll just give me a minute here. I thought I was done with what I was doing, but now I get this email from somebody. This won't take long."

The next ten minutes no doubt fly by in Alan's reckoning, fingers whizzing across the laptop keyboard, alternately humming and whistling to himself, alternately intoning *what?* and *oh my god* to himself like clockwork every thirty seconds. Natalie might have already put her nosedive plan into action if she thought she could find a window before the much-anticipated blizzard in hell.

When he finally looks up at her and lowers the screen on his laptop, she notices that the hairless testicle seems to have ascended somewhat.

"So, what can I do for you this time, Natalie, my dear customer?" The chirpiness in his voice is betrayed by the steadiness in his eyes, the wetness of his lips.

"I need you to find someone for me. You are familiar with the scandal involving Senator Bergman, I am sure?"

"Oh yes, the next Bill Clinton is very much on my radar. I know you've been following him too. I've been enjoying your articles. So enchantingly wicked."

"Well, be that as it may. My boss, as usual, is less impressed. She wants me to get the angle of the female half of the scandal."

"Ah, yes, the Lewinski component. I haven't heard a thing about her since the first reports came out."

"Neither has anyone else. That's why Karin wants us to be the first ones."

"The girl was a Fantasies companion, yes? That's why nobody knows who she was. She could have a new face *and* body by now."

"That's why I need you—if I'm to have any chance of finding her."

"I'd need to have at least one picture of her from the event."

Natalie has already pulled out her phone and dragged up the image. There are still about five feet between herself and Alan, enough to justify him, in his mind at least, in squinting toward it and saying, "I can hardly see from here. You'll have to come closer. Come to think of it, can I offer you a seat?" He shoves the remnants of a Domino's pizza and a host of smaller miscellanea off the cushion next to him and slaps the leather with his palm, struggling mightily to keep his features merely politely inviting.

The testicle has completely disappeared by now.

Might as well get it over with.

She settles her bony rump onto the cushion after slipping on a come-sprinkled magazine and nearly denting her face on the massive laptop. Alan is careful to caress the back of her hand as he lifts the phone from it.

"Well, well, well. Talk about a real Larsen's beauty. That's your all-American Aphrodite, bought and paid for. I never knew the senator had such good taste."

Alan continues in this vein for quite some time, increasingly to himself as the screen inches its way closer to his eyes. The one good thing about his landfill of an apartment is that the multitude of distractions serves to distance Natalie from her own, generating an overload that leads to a sort of mental lockdown. For the first time in days, particularly these last few days, she is beginning to feel calm.

The newfound tranquility allows her to form a proper mental image. Upon some reflection, she decides to challenge herself and goes with Erin. The agitation that so plagued her in the car raises its head, nervously at first, sniffing at the air around her crotch, growing more certain of itself as she indulges it at last.

Her ankles are halfway to the cushion before Alan lowers the phone.

"Well," he says, hoarsely, coughing, rattling phlegm. "I would be happy to see what I can do. Still, this is going to be a tough job. They don't come much more secretive than a group like Fantasies Inc. They're going to have every firewall known to man between me and your girl."

"That's why I came to you. You are the best, my Alan."

He likes it when she calls him that. He has never said so, but she can see it in his eyes. When he hands the phone back to her, she is careful to let her touch linger on his palm, sweaty and sticky already, feeling his pulse jump.

"I am the best, but I'm going to need some collateral. You know what I mean."

"I do know what you mean. Being but a humble journalist, I cannot afford to pay you properly in dollars and cents. I have only one other treasure to offer."

It is all she can do to keep from bursting into hilarity when she uses that fluttery voice, but it is worth it to see him licking his lips, face flushing, mouth twitching, hands trembling. Is the laptop rising an inch already off his lap?

"You understand that I would never ask it of you if you were unable to pay, we could simply both move on with our lives ..."

"Alan, I know you are a gentleman, but let's cut the foreplay. I'm a busy woman."

Fine with him, evidently. The laptop cruises to the ground across a mountain slope of wrappers and glossy magazine covers as he twists to face her, the bulge in the front of his boxers scarcely sufficing to contain the plunderer within.

She pushes him backward until their positions are reversed, she on top for once, he prone beneath her, caught entirely off guard.

From this angle, he could be taken to look slightly like Erin. He is fleshy enough, and she has always thought that the prettiest women would look like men if you shaved off all the hair on their heads.

Hope you like it down there, Erin, because once I've got you on your back, you're never getting that ass off the ground again.

She is not sure if she gasps Erin's name as she collapses, as the dampness spreads. If she did, he probably took no notice. There are many things in Alan's eyes right now, but comprehension is not one of them. She notices his left hand fumbling at her hair, no, stroking it, and is surprised when she realizes she wants to cry.

Not for herself, of course. For the pathetic creature beneath her. For his place in her life, and for her place in his. For the hellish spiderweb that brought them together, and binds them in this ugly state. Why must there be lives like this, like her own, like Alan's, is a mystery she does not care to contemplate.

The closest thing to an answer, the only thing that comes readily to mind, is not so much that there is no god, but rather, that is there is one, he just might be the devil.

★　★　★

"Hello?"

"Hello, is this Jasmin Corker?"

"Yes." The extended drawl conveys the impression that the woman has been asked this question too many times.

"Good morning, Mrs. Corker. My name is Natalie Schroder. I'm an investigative journalist. Your late husband and I were acquainted through work."

"I see."

Natalie waits for the other woman to continue. She does not.

"Look, I'm investigating a story related to some of your late husband's work, so I wonder if we could meet. There are some questions I would like to ask you and—"

"Ben never talked to me about his work. That's probably why I'm still alive."

Natalie is mildly surprised to realize that the other woman's voice is African American. She is even more surprised that it took her so long to notice.

"Well, be that as it may, Mrs. Corker, I know your husband kept many handwritten notes during his investigations. Do you still have his notebooks, or anything else that might be … of use … in getting to the bottom of—"

"Does this have to do with that Fantasies corporation, whatever the hell they're called—what Ben was working on when they killed him?"

The bluntness of the question is nothing compared to the deadpan voice in which it is delivered, no question mark at the end.

"As a matter of fact, it does, Mrs. Corker. I hope you understand that I don't mean to intrude on your grief or on your husband's memory. I am certainly not trying to exploit his work. I am simply—"

"What kind of an idiot are you? You know what they did to Ben, don't you?"

"Yes, Mrs. Corker, I do. I am well aware of the dangers." She rushes her words a bit, simply to have the satisfaction of completing a sentence uninterrupted.

The widow, however, finally seems to have run out of snark. She breathes heavily through the line for a moment and then, from the way her breath seems to reverberate in and out, Natalie can tell she is nodding. "Well, if you don't mind getting fed to the fishes, who am I to say no? Let's see, can you come by … say, four in the afternoon, tomorrow?"

Mrs. Corker gives an address in Renton. Natalie already has an appointment scheduled with a political professor in Tacoma at five thirty, but she is willing to risk the latter.

"I'll be there, Mrs. Corker. Thank you so very much!"

The widow hangs up without another word. The silence of the severed phone connection washes over Natalie like a watery grave.

★   ★   ★

Jasmin Corker lives on the wrong side of the tracks.

Literally, as it transpires.

To reach the widow's home, Natalie has to cross the train tracks that run parallel to I-5 almost immediately after getting off the Corson Avenue exit, rattling through a mangled intersection and nearly missing the necessary right turn a mere half a block past the tracks.

The tiny duplex is situated at the corner of a block packed tight with cheap new developments, the sort of neighborhood that is situated unexpectedly among the utilitarian corporate wastes around it, blending into the wasteland, taking the interloper by surprise with the realization that they are, in fact, surrounded by inhabited dwellings.

You could ambush an entire army here, and nobody would ever know the difference.

The Corkers' half of the house, the lower half of the two-story structure, is as squalid and blue as the other half, squeezed onto a property so small there is no driveway, just the semblance of a lawn that ends abruptly at the sidewalk, less than five feet from the two stone steps leading up to the front door. A fence comprised of planks clumsily wired together rings the property, each plank an inch wide and perhaps a millimeter thick, perhaps an entire foot of space separating the fence from the north and east exterior walls of the house. The other two walls face out onto the sidewalk. Every square foot of the property not taken up by the house and the steps, the pitiful lawn too small to spread a blanket, is choked with weeds, some of them reaching up almost to the ground-floor windows.

Ben Corker may have been a fool, but he deserved better than this.

Jasmin Corker opens the door after what seems like too few knocks. The formidable expression on her broad dark face is only somewhat diminished by the fact that she is wearing a massive mustard yellow sweater and apparently nothing else—not to worry, it comes all the way down to her knees, leaving visible only two brown calves, each the size of an antique umbrella holder.

"Mrs. Corker?"

"You must be Mrs. Schroder."

"*Miss* Schroder, yes."

"Whatever. Yes, please do come in."

The sizable woman turns and leads Natalie into a dilapidated living room, distinguished by gray wallpaper and a thirty-year-old curve-screened television.

"I hope you'll forgive my attire," Mrs. Corker says, shuffling left toward the kitchen (a mere extension of the living room) where a mountain of dishes waits in the sink. "I work all night at Virginia Mason, get back just in time to take the kids to school, and then I come back here and sleep until it's time to pick them up."

Quite how that explains the mystery of her undress, Natalie is not quite sure, but she thinks better of pursuing that thread. Instead, she gets down to business. "Thank you for letting me come here, Mrs. Corker. I don't want to take up any more of your time than I have to, so if you could—"

"Oh, don't worry about that," the widow says, waving a large hand airily, taking up her place in front of the sink. "I got all the time in the world. My day is just starting."

Sigh. "Well, thank you, Mrs. Corker. I appreciate your generosity enormously. Unfortunately, I am on a rather tight schedule, so if you wouldn't mind …"

"So, you say you knew Ben?" Her voice has turned sharp now. A penetrating brown eye rests on Natalie from over a yellow-clad shoulder.

"We were acquainted, yes. Working as we did in similar fields, we moved through some of the same circles. He struck me as a, how shall I say, the sort of man who would be a handful at the best of times, but a fine journalist of course."

Mrs. Corker lets out a light snort and turns her attention back to the dishes. "Oh, he was that, all right. *A handful at the best of times.* I couldn't have put it better myself. My, oh my, oh my." She scrapes determinedly at a stubborn patch of gravy on a frying pan while the muffled sound of two young voices, one distinctly feminine, the other less determinate, reaches Natalie's ears. The dinginess of the place must be affecting Natalie more than she had realized because a sudden surge of maternal pity wells up in her chest at the sound. She wonders suddenly whether the surge in property tax rates predicted in the case of the arms bill passing will leave the Corkers able to afford their home. Her stomach twists ever tighter in discomfort. Simply to get her mind away from the subject, not caring much about the answer, she hears herself asking, "I don't suppose you know what your husband was working on when he … when it happened?"

The widow's scrubbing slows for a moment, just a moment. "Ben never talked to me about his work. No, that was on a need-to-know basis as far as he was concerned. Fine with me. I didn't want to know anyway, but it didn't seem like a good idea to be knowing too much about that shit. Definitely for the best, as it turned out."

Natalie has felt more than one chill creeping down her spine lately, but this one is perhaps the most heartless. She is on the verge of opening her mouth to raise the subject of why she came again when the other woman continues.

"I only ever met one of his associates. I remember his name because it seemed so funny to me, Billy Twombly. Is that a white boy name—or is that a white boy name? Anyways, I never did know what they were doing together, but Ben invited him over here for dinner about a month before, you know, all hell broke loose.

Strange fellow. Real geek, you could tell just looking at him. Can't say that I liked the look of him much, but Ben seemed to like him, more's the mystery."

The reference to the chronology is the only thing that catches Natalie's attention, but it is enough to lead her to repeat the name several times rapidly to herself.

A loud wail suddenly fills the living space, eventually coalescing into the ubiquitous cry of "Mommy!"

"Oh, for heaven's sake. Excuse me for a moment." Mrs. Corker drops her rag in the sink and bustles toward the hallway that Natalie had not noticed in the east wall until now. As soon as the other woman is around the corner, Natalie pulls out her phone and types the name into her notes.

Rocking back and forth between her heels and the balls of her feet as Mrs. Corker's scolding voice emanates from the children's bedroom, Natalie can feel the familiar vise beginning to press itself on her temples as her impatience builds. Fortunately, when the widow reemerges, she looks frazzled enough to want to get her guest out of the house.

"Let me see, you were after what my husband left, weren't you? I'm sorry if I've been keeping you, Miss uh, Miss Schroder. As you can see, I'm just about at the end of my wits here."

"I quite understand."

"Follow me please." Mrs. Corker heads down the tiny hallway with two doors on either side and one at the end. It is to this third that the widow leads her.

The room is dusty and almost empty. A chest of drawers lines the north wall, an empty bed frames the south, and the only distinguishing feature of the east wall is a window with a fine view of the gray fence a foot beyond it.

"I'm afraid I had to sell Ben's computer. It was password protected, of course, so you might not have been able to use it anyway, but I needed the money. He didn't leave a whole lot. His phone went missing when he did, and it never came back—not even as a corpse." Mrs. Corker lets out a laugh rather like a hyena's bark as she pulls open the top drawer of the chest.

"This is all I can think of," the widow says, pulling out an ancient-looking one-subject seventy-page college-ruled notebook. The pages are yellowed with age. "That might be of some help to you. He used to scribble things down in this when he was looking for connections between things. I never knew what that meant, but he said it helped him to think about certain things, to take it down by hand. He was doing that a lot, right around the end."

"Thank you. Thank you very much." Natalie takes the notebook with trembling hands, not daring to open it just yet.

"Not a problem, Mrs. Schroder, sorry, *Miss* Schroder. I don't suppose you have any kids, do you?" Jasmin Corker is already leading her out of the room, but she looks inquisitively at Natalie when she hesitates to answer.

"No, I'm afraid I don't." The distinctive sound of a little boy smashing two action figures together emerges from the rightward door as Natalie passes it, followed closely by an unintelligible female squeal from the other child.

"Yeah, I didn't think so. I don't blame you. Still, it has its rewards. I don't suppose you ever regretted it?"

"No, I can't say that I ever particularly wanted to."

Mrs. Corker's hand is on the front doorknob, and there is an almost calculating look in her sizable eyes as she gazes back at Natalie, causing the journalist to bristle without quite knowing why.

"If you don't mind me saying, you don't seem like the sort of woman who would like children," the widow finally says.

The words should not wound, but they do, ever so slightly.

"I wouldn't say that I don't like children. I've just never had much time to be around them—not even when I was one," Natalie says, struggling to control her voice.

"What I mean is, it seems like lesbians don't usually like children much, is all I'm saying. Not judging, just how it seems."

Natalie is not sure what to make of that, but she is keener than ever to leave.

"I'm not a lesbian. I'd have to be a woman. If you don't mind, Mrs. Corker."

"You're not saying that you're a man in a woman's body, are you?"

"Not exactly, no. Not that it would be anyone's business if I was." Oh yes, a touch of acid is dripping into her tone now.

"I'm sorry, I don't mean any offense. Honestly, I find that sort of thing kind of interesting. You know, my brother, a few years back, decided that he had always been a woman on the inside. So, he starts dressing like a woman, talking like a woman, but he doesn't get a sex change. Still has a penis, but he says he's a woman. All this only after going to college, you know, bunch of liberals. I don't understand people."

She has a point there, Natalie must concede. "I know exactly what you mean, Mrs. Corker. Thank you very much again for your generosity. I'm sure your late husband's notes will be very helpful to me."

Her face is still halfway turned away from the other woman, partway out the door, one foot on the top step, awkwardly poised between the conflicting desires to leave and to leave without being rude, when she feels the familiar, clingy strands of a spiderweb catching at her face.

Natalie lurches away from the sensation even as the momentum of her step carries her forward. The result is that she stumbles, arms waving, strands of the web that stretches from the awning to the step catching in her hands and in her hair. Later, she will wonder how she failed to notice it when she first approached, but in the event, she can think only of the tiny, twitching, brightly colored arachnid body surely crawling across her skin already in the seconds before she strikes the ground, left foot still on the top step, the sky looking close enough to touch.

Pushing herself to her feet, ignoring the obligatory "Are you okay?" from Mrs. Corker, brushing herself off, rubbing her hands over herself as though to be sure that she has not sprained or broken anything, but in reality, endeavoring to sweep away the spiderweb strands and making sure that the arachnid itself is nowhere to be found on her person, Natalie devotes the remaining scraps of her consciousness to controlling her breathing and waiting for her heartbeat to return to normal. It takes a while.

At length, Mrs. Corker repeats, "Are you okay?"

Natalie turns toward her. "Yes. Yes, I'm fine. Thank you. Damned thing came out of nowhere." As though it were a joke.

As the door is closing behind her, the sound of a child's shriek drifts after her once more. Despite the anger that is still threatening to erupt in her veins, another stab of pity fills her. At the thought of living in this hovel, at the thought that soon they might not even have that much.

That's who you're doing this for, she thinks. *If you take down Bergman, they might stand a chance. You really will be a hero. But why does the thought of heroism taste so much like poison?*

★   ★   ★

To say that Ben Corker's notes do not exactly spill their guts at first viewing would be an understatement—though not for any wont of guts to be spilt.

Into every single inch of space in the pages of the notebook, Corker managed to cram the stream of consciousness that carried him through twenty years of investigative journalism. Natalie can tell. Indecipherable though much of it is, even though at least half of it has been crossed out, while the rest of it never amounts to more than a couple of phrases strung together in haphazard combinations, she is sufficiently familiar with Corker's body of work to recognize certain names, places, and figures from the early pages of the notebook as correlating with his earliest career.

She flips to the back of the notebook, and she finds the sprawling web of his last case spread over the final three pages, front and back, each page less legible than the one before it.

There must be something to the concept of karma after all. Though what could I have done even in another life to have deserved this?

Sapphire hops up onto the couch next to her and buries his face in her hip. The contended purr serves to marginally soothe Natalie's nerves as she scratches him between the ears with one hand while tracing the lines of the notebook with the other.

There is no telling where to begin. *Beginning*, of course, is an irrelevant term when it comes to a stream of consciousness.

A circle is round, it has no end, that's why I don't want to be your friend.

It does not take long for certain names to start leaping out at her, scribbled in blue pen, names familiar from Corker's articles and the articles of others, one or two of them her own. Once the names start to fall into place, then the assorted initials, abbreviations, and connecting arrows start to make more sense—even without knowing always what they refer to.

Jupiter Strong. JS. Giulio Visconti. GV. Jules Reich. JR.

Those are the ones she knows. Less readily understood are the initials *DE* and *EH,* which appear more than once without any accompanying full name. The only unknown full name to appear is Darryl Eaton, which appears in close conjunction with what appears to be a company name: *Eaton's Evaluations.* That there are plenty more initials and abbreviations that appear in isolation goes without saying.

Even more confusing are the phrases with which they intersect:

DE = JS (?)
EH = TC (?)
Fantasies = EE (?)
Catalina = VO (?)
Catalina = RK
JS = OL
Daphne R = Jacqueline
Domina J = Odalisque

On and on the scribblings go, blending into one another, fading around corners and sometimes disappearing, constantly framed by crossings-out and question marks and arrows and bullet points. Sapphire has fallen asleep in Natalie's lap, and her head is on the verge of splitting down the middle when Billy Twombly's name floats inexplicably into her mind.

In the dim lamplight of her living room, staring at the bookshelves that face the couch, Natalie pulls out her phone and hesitates. She could try to research the name under her own steam, but she does not have much of that left. Besides, there is a good chance that Alan will already be familiar with it.

"Natalie, what the hell do you want?"

"Good evening to you too, Alan. Are you busy?"

"Extremely, as you know very well, you who just gave me the hardest job of my life to do here."

"Well, that sounds lovely, Alan, so lovely that I wonder if I could interrupt you for a moment to ask you a question."

"It better be a damn good question, Natalie. I've already got swimmers here."

"Well, it's sort of a multipronged question. First off, do you know anything about a company called Eaton's Evaluations?"

Silence greets her for a moment. From the eventual answer, she deduces that it was a stunned silence.

"Are you kidding me? You never heard of Eaton's?"

"I may have heard the name before, but I never gave it much thought."

"I mean, Jesus, Natalie, they're only the most expensive information research company in the country. Based in Seattle, naturally, up on Beacon Hill."

"An information research company … what does that mean, exactly?"

"Like, you pay them to do online research for you, and they do it—for a hefty sum. Conduct polls, market analysis, that sort of thing. Dangerously accurate, like 96 percent accuracy rates. Very impressive."

"Wait a minute. You say they conduct *polls?* Market analysis? That's it?"

"Oh, it's a lot more than that. They can do just about anything. The guy who started it, that Darryl Eaton, he's an old college friend of Ole Larsen. University of Copenhagen. He's like a genius psychoanalyst. He designs these surveys, and they're not just surveys but algorithms, complex studies, all kinds of things, to figure out how masses of people feel about different things."

"I can see how that could be useful in market analysis. But, I mean, you said they're accurate up to *96 percent* of the time?"

"Oh, hell yeah. Like I say, this Eaton, he's a psychological genius, for real. He knows how to word these polls so that he can tell even how honest a person is being with their answers, all sorts of things. He knows how to assess what kinds of people are answering his polls and what that says about the sorts of people who don't respond to polls, how that factors in, all very precise."

"So ... does this, um, information company have any links to Fantasies that you know of? Or to Bergman or anything?"

"I don't know specifically, but I'd be more surprised if they didn't. Just about every corporation you can think of has gone to Eaton's for market analysis in the last ten years, and they have plenty of other rich clients. I've heard about a lot of politicians, government agencies, and other things taking advantage of their services. The Department of Transportation is one of their biggest clients, apparently. They keep it pretty hushed up, of course, but any political candidate with enough money is well advised to use Eaton's services. I'd be surprised if Bergman hadn't gone to them for help over the years. They make the most money in states where the two parties are the most evenly matched, both desperate for an edge. They only make about half as much in states like this—where the Democratic majority doesn't need them so much. It's the Republicans who have to spend all their money just trying to get a leg up."

"I see. And so, these services are perfectly legal, like, legit?"

"For the most part. They got in some trouble a couple years ago. The DA tried to prosecute them for, oh, I don't know what all, let's see ... well, it was the usual sort of things you would expect from that sort of web-based company, you know, paying social media websites for their users' information, peddling information they weren't supposed to have or weren't supposed to divulge, all that fun stuff. Oh, and I think they accused them of setting up some fake blogs, accounts on various social media sites, using these pages to conduct experiments, you know, by gauging how certain people responded to certain types of posts, that sort of thing."

"Kind of like the Russian hackers, back in the day."

"Exactly like that."

"So, what happened with the DA?"

"Oh, the usual story, not enough evidence, blah blah blah. Eventually they got a slap on the wrist, and then Governor Reich said they didn't even have to pay it."

Governor Reich again. Strand by strand, the spiderweb begins to piece itself together behind Natalie's eyes, the invisible nightmare shape of the arachnid hovering in the shadows around the edge.

"I think I'm beginning to see where this is going. Now, here's the second part of my inquiry: Have you ever heard of someone called Billy Twombly?"

Later, she will almost swear she heard Alan snort at the mention of the name.

"As a matter of fact, yes, dear. William Twombly ties in quite neatly with our discussion of Eaton's Evaluations. You see, up until quite recently, he was the branch manager of the Seattle branch of the company, the most important branch. Not exactly the second-in-command under Eaton himself, but high up there."

"Up until quite recently, you said."

"Yes. You see, last year, when all that trouble was going on—you know, with Reich and everyone else—well, Eaton's was one of the corporations accused of having links to the Mafia, to Reich, and so on and so forth. Nothing substantial, not even enough for another attempt at prosecution, but there was some evidence of cooperation. Executive meetings, nothing you haven't heard a million times. So anyway, you know the story: Reich resigns, everything simmers down, and then, all of a sudden, this William Twombly, one of Eaton's top executives, announces his retirement and disappears."

"He disappeared? Like, right off the map?"

"Oh, no, Natalie, no, not off the map at all. That's the funniest part. You see, this guys at the peak of his career, raking in millions a year, and suddenly he announces he's done. And the company, they don't hold it against him. In fact, they pay him a substantial pension to go into exile. So, he retires, leaves his wife and ten-year-old daughter at home, and moves down to California. Lives there on a beachfront, holding a party all night, every night."

"Almost as though they were paying him to keep something to himself."

"That was the general consensus among the few people to know about it."

"Well, thank you very much, Alan. I'll let you get back to your fun evening."

She presses the red dot before Alan can beg for phone sex. Setting the phone down on the cushion beside her with a sigh, Natalie leans her head back on the couch and squeezes her eyes shut. It is going to be another long night.

Fortunately, there is no time like the present. It takes some searching to find the number, but Alan was correct. It is a California number.

"Hello?" The voice is gravelly, the sound of sand made air. It is not the voice you would expect from a computer geek, even one who lives at the beach.

"Hello, is this William Twombly?" She already knows it is his house; there is indeed the sound of a raucous party reverberating through the phone connection.

"Yes, it is. May I ask who I'm speaking with?" Clearly impatient, probably thinking, *This is exactly what I moved to California to escape!*

"My name is Natalie Schroder. I'm an investigative journalist …"

"Hold on … quiet down over there! Wait, you said you're Natalie Schroder? From Seattle? Aren't you the one who wrote that really nasty story about Owen Caldwell?"

"Yes, that's me." She is mildly surprised that he knows who she is. "Look, Mr. Twombly, I don't want to distract you from your gathering. I only have one question to ask you … if you don't mind?"

A sigh rasps through the line. "Well, make it quick, please."

"Thank you. Mr. Twombly, do you by any chance know the name of the girl who was assaulted by Senator Milton Bergman in the Seashell Hotel recently?"

For what feels like the better part of a full minute, there is no answer save the thudding rock music, the laughs, and the girlish shrieks from the other end of the line. Then Billy Twombly lets out a formidable thump of a breath, says, "Go fuck yourself, Miss Schroder," and hangs up.

Well, at least that went better than I expected.

Sapphire wakes up as she is returning her phone to her pocket. With a soft mewl, he begs for her hand. She obliges him, tracing her palm all the way from his ears to the base of his tail, and then returning it to rub her fingertips between his ears.

As the cat's purr reverberates from his chest up her arm and into her own chest, an image fills her mind: a sort of composite face that looks at first like Erin Hopkins and then morphs into Alan.

As the purring mounts, it occurs to Natalie, not for the first time, that the best way to teach boys to give girls sexual pleasure would be to give them a cat and teach them to make it purr.

She wonders if Alan would appreciate a cat. She is surprised to realize how much she cares about the answer to a question she will never ask him.

CHAPTER SIX

"CLARISSA! WELCOME HOME!"

"Hi, Dad!"

The senator's daughter rushes into the senator's arms, and the senator's wife rolls her eyes in the doorway, two of her daughter's bags hanging from her shoulders, disgusted apparently by the very existence of affection directed toward her husband.

They already dropped Miranda off at her parents' house across the street. Vanessa has long been in the habit of picking up the girls at the airport when they come back from Virginia. She is always careful to deposit Miranda at home before unloading her own daughter.

Fortunately, Vanessa is scheduled to attend one of her ridiculous social gatherings tonight, a group of a dozen comparably aged married women sitting in a circle of comfy chairs in the corner of a coffee shop somewhere, discussing Sartre and Beauvoir and whatever other French fruits are on the menu.

In the meantime, the senator has an appointment to make. The limo is already waiting in the driveway, blocking the entire entrance. Maybe that's why Vanessa is still looking daggers at him. She and Clarissa have subsequently been forced to drag the latter's possessions across fifty yards of lawn. Which, in and of itself, is enough to justify the purchase of a limo, as far as Milton is concerned.

"Pass all your classes?"

"I think so."

"You *think* so, do you?"

"Well, history and women's studies, I'm positive. Biology—"

"Think you can get Terrence to move the fucking limo?" Vanessa has not moved an inch, but her fury is protruding palpably into the mansion.

"I'll get the rest of the bags; don't worry." Milton sighs, releases Clarissa, and moves toward the door.

Vanessa does not immediately stand aside. "Why is the limo out anyway?"

"I'm sitting on a panel for KOMO 4, to debate the arms bill. I told you."

She snorts in disgust, evidently remembering the words he muttered to her that morning in the library after all, and stomps away from him. Clarissa and Milton simultaneously mime nagging before the girl follows in her mother's wake.

Halfway across the lawn, the last two heavy bags in his arms, he comes to a halt, sun-drunk in the suddenly blazing heat, now that the sun has come fully out. The exhaustion stems from more than the heat. The cumulus that drifts around the fiery disc is as ephemeral as life. He knows this suddenly, and yet, as the fragrances of pollen and earth fill his nostrils inescapably, Milton Bergman almost feels as though he might live forever.

Female Associates Defend Bergman
by Natalie Schroder
June 14, 20—

In the weeks since Senator Milton Bergman (R-WA) was released from custody after what has been taken as an illicit (and illegal) hotel tryst gone horribly wrong, the controversial politician has been embattled from all sides with accusations of sexism, misogyny, and generally perpetuating the abuse of power by privileged white men.

"There is nothing surprising about this behavior, which makes it all the more shocking," says Kylie Moffat, thirty-nine, a Seattle victims' advocate and behavioral therapist.

But one group of women has remained surprisingly supportive of the Republican senator: his closest female associates.

"I have known [Senator Bergman] for many years now, and I refuse to believe that he was up to any wrongdoing in that hotel that night," said Heidi Bates, a longtime staffer and personal friend of the senator, who went on to refer to Bergman as "an embodiment of everything his party, his church, and his worldview stands for."

In a similar vein, Phyllis Jenkins, a lawyer who worked alongside Bergman for two years at the legal firm Kaufman and Harding at the beginning of both their careers more than twenty years ago and a lifelong Democrat, has likewise defended her former colleague against accusations of sexism, in his personal, professional, and private life, accusing Bergman's vilifiers of what she calls "politicized outrage."

"Anyone who has known Milton knows that he is not a sexist pig or a right-wing bigot," said Jenkins. "He is a fundamentally good person at heart; anyone could see that if they spoke to him for any length of time."

Jenkins went on to say, "Seattle loves to hate Bergman for obvious partisan reasons. In their rush to condemn his supposed anti-woman agenda, they forget, almost deliberately, that Bergman has always voted in favor of women's reproductive rights, for legislation to combat sexual harassment and inequality, closing the pay gap. He is the most liberal Republican in his party, more of a libertarian than a conservative, in truth."

Jenkins concluded, "Seattle has become a bastion of what I consider a form of left-wing bigotry, all the more hypocritical because it would be the first to claim that it despises bigotry in all forms. Only a bigot would look at a case as broad as that leveled against Bergman, you know, *he's a sexist pig* and everything, supported by so little evidence, and call any scrap of evidence conclusive proof. That is at least as despicable as what the man is being accused of."

"What the *hell* is this?" Karin's voice shatters the silence of Natalie's cubicle, punctuated by the sound of a newspaper, open to the page containing her newest article, slapping down on her desk.

Natalie slowly pries her gaze away from the computer screen covered with a satellite map of Seattle, zeroed in on the headquarters of Eaton's Evaluations, and turns her attention to the paper: *Female Associates Defend Bergman.*

"What is this? What is this? Well, aren't you the riddler, Karin? Let me see if I can figure this one out."

"Don't bother. I've got a better one for you—a riddle that has even me stumped. Here's how it goes: Why would anyone, much less any woman, or what passes for a woman, write an article all about women who love Milton Bergman?"

"I don't know if they *love* him exactly."

"Oh, Senator Bergman is so kind? Senator Bergman is so not a sexist? All he does is cheat on his wife and beat up hookers and—"

"Oh, Karin, if that's all it takes to make a person a sexist pig, who isn't?"

"And of course you would find Phyllis Jenkins, the woman who has gotten no less than thirteen men off of sexual assault charges."

"I suppose now they're not even entitled to a legal defense? Someone accuses somebody, send them straight to prison forever?"

That one finally cuts through Karin's seething. Catching her breath, she glares at Natalie, placing her hands on her hips.

"Natalie, you are entitled to your own perspective, of course, but this is going too far. To have published this without my permission—"

"Without your permission? You had to okay it before it went out!"

"You turned it in late—I can't help suspecting deliberately—so that I had no choice. It would have fucked up the formatting otherwise, as you very well know."

"Oh *no*. It would have fucked up the formatting? Oh my god. Whatever could you have done, Karin? I feel so sorry for you now."

"Shut up, Natalie! Do you understand me?" A dangerous note has entered Karin's voice now, one that Natalie has sensed her striving for in the past but has never quite reached—until now. "I am not going to threaten you, because I do not choose to be that kind of boss. You know as well as I do where we stand. That's all you should need to know. Where we go from here is up to you." Karin turns and strides away without another word, without giving Natalie time to respond.

Just as well. Natalie is not sure quite what she would have said, but *too far* would undoubtedly be too mild a term for where it would have taken them. There is too much on her mind for Karin's feeble warnings to trouble her much in any case. As she turns her attention back to the computer screen, she exits out of the satellite image and returns to another header, the one containing her Google search for William Twombly, Eaton's Evaluations. Several photographs line the screen above his personal information, the former showing a surprisingly handsome, tanned face on which a pair of wire-rimmed spectacles look strange, the latter detailing a formidable list of degrees and accolades.

And to think that raspy voice came out of this face.

A rustling at her back distracts her. The sound of the steps reminds her of Karin, and she whirls around in her swivel chair with a snarl forming on her lips.

Only to be caught off guard by the nervous face of Marla.

"Oh … hello, Marla," she says, sounding sheepish.

"Good morning, Natalie." For once, the girl sounds not brightly, falsely chirpy but rather nervous. Then Natalie notices the envelope in her hands. "This, uh, this came for you in this morning's mail. No return address. Karin insisted on having it bomb-sniffed."

I guess we know she didn't send it then. "I understand. Well, thank you, Marla."

She turns the white envelope over in her hands until the girl has disappeared, taking in the blocky handwriting at dead center, stating only her name and the office address. The precision of that handwriting makes her think of a computer.

Natalie is annoyed to notice her hands shaking as she opens the envelope, pulling out a single piece of folded white paper on which has been printed, in the same handwriting:

> multidimensional eruditions exaggerate topographical philistinisms, hexagonal imitations liquidating indigenous participles galvanized ontologically loquacious, defenestrating insipid notaries gloating anciently, tertiary billiards owing renegades intricate selections toward avuncular verticals, every rotation negating serpentine ellipticals, venal epaulettes notified, protracted militants tenaciously multiplying omnipresent rebellious reactionary orca whales, torpidly wriggling ossified mountains belying lucid yachts

She is not sure how many minutes have passed when she realizes that she is gazing at the paper with her mouth hanging open.

Clamping her jaw tight shut, Natalie spins around and examines the paper with the glare of the computer screen as a backdrop. It may be simply because of the sight of the name Twombly on the screen behind the paper that she notices the first letters of the last two words in the sequences, that it dawns on her so quickly that it is a simple anagram, which she interprets as:

Meet Philip Golding at Boris Tavern 7pm tomorrow Twombly

★ ★ ★

"Senator Bergman, you've not spoken so far. Could we get your input? What do you think the effect of the arms bill would be on the national debt?" Valerie Wells does not quite meet his eye as she speaks; her voice sort of trails off at the end rather than rising on the question mark.

"Well, Valerie, I think it's safe to say that investing in a business as consistently lucrative as arms and weapons could not possibly explode the national debt, contrary to what my colleague Senator Demetrio seems to think. In the ten years since Sheridan slashed the defense budget in half, we have seen no decrease in the national debt, quite the opposite of what we were promised. Furthermore—"

"Valerie, if I could interject here," says Chloe Demetrio, situated as far to the right of Milton as possible (there are six of them on the panel, in order from right to left, three Democrats, Senator Demetrio, Congressman Wallace Steward, and mayor of Seattle George Joyce, and three Republicans,

Port Commissioner Philip Kingston, Bergman, and Congresswoman Carolyn Bulk), "President Sheridan never promised that the reduction of the defense budget would implode the national debt, rather that it would contribute to reducing the debt's expansion, and if the famously reliable Senator Bergman cared to check the figures, no pun intended, he would see—"

"Chloe, er, Senator Demetrio, I highly resent that comment on my character. Whatever else you may think of me, this is neither the time nor the place—"

"Indeed, it is not, Senator." Valerie's voice, as crisp and sharp as the blonde woman's own stiletto heels, cracks through the exchange. "We are here to discuss the plan for the arms bill. According to several highly regarded analysts, the wording of the proposal as it stands at present is promising to expand the defense budget by more than $600 billion. Now I put it to Senator Bergman, because we've heard so little from you so far, and because, of everyone on the panel, you have been the most vocal champion of this proposal, do you truly feel that a $600 billion investment does not potentially threaten a vast growth of the national debt? In order for it not to do so, would the government not be forced to make unprecedented cuts to social programs, already considered underfunded even after President Sheridan's efforts at reform in that area?"

Congresswoman Bulk, a wispy woman with gray hair and grayer skin, inhales sharply, a gesture noticed by no one but Bergman.

"Valerie, I think if you look a bit more closely at the wording of the proposal in question, you will find that the $600 billion allocated to national defense is not allotted specifically to the Department of Defense. It is designed to benefit arms manufacturers, researchers in a wide variety of scientific fields, federal contractors at multiple levels, all good-paying, expanding job fields who will not only be able to grow the American workforce with the money in question—"

"*Some* of the money in question," Bulk mutters through pouting lips.

"It will also repay the money within five years at a 15 percent profit margin to quote several leading economists and market analysts."

"Valerie, could I respond to that?" Wallace Steward looks more like a Caucasian basketball player than a politician, a six-foot-three tower of a man. He even has a broken nose to complete the illusion.

"Please, Congressman, go ahead."

"Senator Bergman, I have no doubt that well over $600 billion will be returned in profits. But who will profit from those profits? Will those profits go straight into the hands of the taxpayers who supplied the original investment —or will it go straight into the pockets of the military industrial complex while thirty million women and children beg for crumbs on the streets because they lost their welfare?"

"The money will come back to them," says Philip Kingston, as slow and patient in speech as his advance up the political ladder. He is by far the oldest person on the panel, a month short of eighty. "When employers are once again able to pay their employees properly, provide them with decent benefits, when the profits derived from the investment are taxed to provide them with their precious social programs—"

"Why not just keep paying for their social programs, if that's what you're after?" blares George Joyce, a short, round man with a mustache as black and bristly as his temper. "Tax a 15 percent profit, probably not even that much, that'll make up for cutting $600 *billion* from public spending?"

"Mayor, please, let's keep this from turning into a free-for-all," Valerie says in the pacifying tone of a kindergarten teacher. "Congresswoman Bulk, I thought I noticed a trace of dissension in your face a moment ago. Compared to your Republican colleagues, you have been more muted in your support for the bill, or so it seems."

"You see, Valerie, while I agree with the expansion of the defense budget and the investment in armaments—in principle, that is—I am also inclined to agree with some of what my liberal colleagues have been saying with regard to the debt and social programs, more specifically with regard to the sheer *size* of the reallocation—"

"That's interesting, Congresswoman. Because, as currently the only African American female Republican in the House of Representatives, you have consistently defined yourself as a dead-center moderate, frequently crossing party lines on votes concerning economic issues. Yet you continue to caucus as a conservative."

"I am an old-fashioned woman. I don't like abortion. I wish religion played a larger role in public life. I believe when a country reaches its carrying capacity, it has to keep an eye on its borders. I would like for a lot of things to go back to the way they used to be in this country, when I was younger and before I was born. Jim Crow is not one of the things I want to see come back. On that and many other subjects, I am definitely not without a liberal side. I consider myself a Republican because I have more confidence in things as they have been than in ideas for how things could be, if only everything were perfect. There was a time when a United States senator could not have fooled around with a hooker in some sleazy hotel and gotten away with it by telling a bald-faced lie on live television that wouldn't have fooled my uncle when he was high on paint fumes!"

Chloe Demetrio is the first to laugh—and the loudest. The laughs that come after are almost as much at her hilarity as at the words of Congresswoman Bulk. Even Senator Bergman joins in laughing. At Demetrio, not Bulk.

"Thank you, Congresswoman," Valerie Wells says with some difficulty, struggling to keep the laughter out of her own demeanor. "Thank you for reminding us that there is still such a thing as a middle ground in American politics."

The newswoman clears her throat and fidgets with the papers in her hands. "Let's see." She looks Bergman full in the face for the first time. "Well, thank you very much, all of you. It has certainly been a lively discussion. We've just about run out of time, but I'm sure our viewers will be grateful to have your words to chew over. Whatever happens when this arms bill is put to the vote, I hope those of you who will be voting on it, in particular, will remember the value of … conscience."

★   ★   ★

The piece comes on the news precisely as Miranda is exiting the bathroom, clad in a red one-piece swimsuit.

Milton reclines on the king-and-a-half-size bed (extra big for the last ten years to accommodate the ever-growing distance between himself and his wife), already standing at arms, all through the power of memory.

"First, I would like to hear Senator Demetrio's views on …" warbles the voice of Valerie Wells from the seventy-two-inch screen, pixelated to an HD shine so flawless that the woman looks more realistic on the screen than she did in the flesh.

"Oh, Senator, could I please have your views on a subject of the most pressing urgency?" Miranda minces toward the bed doing a spot-on impersonation of the newscaster's voice. Her fleshy body trembles at the edges of the blood-red fabric.

"My dear Miranda, you can have my views on literally any subject, free of charge, on condition that you act as though you agree with them, no matter how controversial they may seem."

She giggles and tiptoes closer, taking her place in the middle of the bed, facing him, blocking the television, three feet beneath his toes. "Senator, I would like to know what a man as intelligent as yourself, as brilliant as yourself, as handsome of yourself, might happen to think of the swimsuit I'm wearing."

"The swimsuit is absolutely perfect. As for the girl whose wearing it, meh."

"Oh, you son of a bitch!" She slaps him playfully on the foot. "I'm going to hurt you for that I'm gonna fuck you up."

"That sounds about right."

"Oh, you *son* of a *bitch*!" She is on her knees between his legs now, shuffling forward, reaching toward him with hands like silk.

"The entire proposal is an absolute joke," Chloe Demetrio is enumerating for the second time today. "McNeil Bohr is neither an economist nor a politician. He is a corporate ventriloquist, and that, frankly, is all you need to know about this bill."

A muffled sound rises from near Milton's crotch, reaching his ears even through the haze that is falling over him. "What was that, dear?"

Miranda disgorges her mouth with some difficulty and says, "I said I can't believe anybody would actually

name their child McNeil. What kind of a first name
is that?"

Milton chuckles for more than one reason. "His
parents named him that so that he could become an
important man someday. Ordinary names go with
ordinary people. That was what my father always told
me. That's why he named me Milton—because he
wanted me to be a somebody. Same thing with McNeil
Bohr, I'm sure."

Miranda contemplates that one for a moment,
shrugs, and returns to what she was doing. *Maybe she'll
give me a son someday, and I'll name him Ambrose, after
my father, or Anselm, after my mother's father.* Wishful
thinking. Maybe not even that.

"If I could respond to Senator Demetrio's
comments," replays the patient wheeze of Philip
Kingston, "I would just like to point out that whatever
she and her friends, these 'leading financial experts'
may believe, I would like to point out that the president
has consulted with a wide variety of economics-related
think tanks, who have played a leading role in the
drafting of this proposal."

The port commissioner's voice dissolves with the
speed of boredom.

The senator's phone vibrates on the bedside table,
five feet away.

Milton is halfway there before he yelps in pain. He
didn't realize he was dragging Miranda along for the
ride until she clamped her jaw in surprise.

"What the hell do you want, Terrence?" Rage and pain combine to make his voice uncharacteristically harsh.

"I just thought you would like to know, sir," says Terrence, sounding taken aback. *Apparently he thought Miranda really was coming over just to visit Clarissa.* "The girl has been taken care of."

"What the hell are you talking about? *Ah.*"

"I knew you'd get there, sir."

"What? No, I sighed because … never mind, what the hell are you talking—"

"The girl, sir." Terrence's voice has taken on the texture of an elementary school teacher, like Valerie Wells on the screen right now. "She has been taken care of."

Miranda's tongue is probing insistently at the base of his shaft when the realization dawns. The sensation jogged a memory.

"Okay, I'm on board now … *oh yeah* … ahem … I see what you're saying … yes, *yes,* that's good to hear … yes that's *so good* to hear … yes, thank you … *thank you!*"

"You're welcome, sir," Terrence says, sounding only mildly disgusted. "Well, I'll let you get back to your—"

Milton presses the red button, cutting his aide off in midsentence. A moment later, Miranda's mouth does the same to Milton's thoughts.

"Senator Bergman, you've not spoken so far."

The familiar sentence jolts Milton out of his reverie before he has properly recovered. That annoys him, though not nearly as much as the way the idiots at

KOMO lit his face, emphasizing the scar on his left cheek. The emotion intensifies, considerably, when he notices that Miranda has picked up and is running her fingertips over the illuminated screen of his phone.

"Hey, *give me that!*" He tugs the device out of her hands and tosses it toward the bedside table. It bounces off the edge and falls to the floor.

"You're back, I see." If Miranda is annoyed by his manhandling, she shows no signs of it, though her eyes are faintly harder than before. That is to be expected, however. She has a way of getting crabby right about now.

"I am. I'm back, I'm loaded, and I'm ready to rumble."

She snorts at the archaisms, but she does not object as he puts his arms around her, holding her close, almost as though he loves her.

"I highly resent that comment on my character …"

"Valerie, if you look a bit more closely at the wording of the proposal …"

Apparently, the struggle didn't kill as much time as it had felt like. Well, what can you do but keep trying. He pulls her closer, trying to concentrate on the sweet smell of her hair, her skin, her body, her youth, tender years tangible in his arms.

"I am an old-fashioned woman. I don't like abortion."

"Oh, for the love of *God!*" Bergman rolls onto his back and buries his face in his palms while Miranda chuckles. He notices her discarded swimsuit down by his feet and contrives to pick it up between his toes, swaying it in front of the television, anything to distract him from the images there, anything to mitigate the roar of laughter that inevitably comes rolling from it.

When the ripple has run its course, Miranda rolls over onto her side and stretches herself half across him, cupping his right cheek in her left hand. By this point, the panel has finally disappeared, Wells has made her final passive-aggressive comments, and the screen has reverted to KOMO 4's political commentators Buck Childe and Vickie Goldman. A middle-aged ginger with the jowls of a man who has lost fifty pounds recently and a face-lifted prune who could use twenty.

"Well, Buck, that sure was an interesting discussion. I was surprised that none of them brought up the comments made recently by Walter Chang, the legal adviser who has suggested that the wording of the proposal as it currently stands would allow military-industrial contractors to expand control of their assets vertically as well as horizontally in the chain of production, which would represent an unprecedented shakedown in the prohibitions against market monopolies."

"I have always said, Vickie, to the champions of the concept of free market capitalism, I point out that to allow people *absolute freedom* is, axiomatically, to allow people the freedom to make slaves of others. In order for capitalism to work, one has to at least regulate the system enough to allow people a degree of individual economic freedom. Some people would say the Republican Party forgot that a long time ago."

Miranda squirms unexpectedly in his arms, whispering gently, "Is that true, Senator? Did the Republican Party forget that a long time ago?"

Milton is in no more mood for games. "Yes," he answers simply, honestly.

★   ★   ★

Natalie's phone buzzes at the precise moment the panel is getting interesting.

"Hello?" *Asshole.*

"What the fuck have you gotten me into, you stupid asshole bitch?"

"Alan, sweetheart, nice to hear your voice."

"Don't give me that shit, Natalie, not tonight, you manipulative *slut!* You might have mentioned that we were fucking with the fucking US government, for fuck's fucking sake!"

"Alan, my precious teacup, I seem to recall mentioning that this entire affair stemmed directly from the mishap involving Senator Bergman."

"I'm not talking about that, you stupid goddamn bitch. We're talking about a branch of the fucking CIA here—I'm goddamn sure of it!"

"Wait, what?" The television is still on, but she never raises the volume high. Her inability to believe her ears stems from elsewhere. "What the hell are you talking about, Alan? What does this have to do with the CIA?"

He seems to be running out of steam, being forced to explain requires him to catch his breath, and the effect is anticlimactic. "Well, I'm not sure if it's the CIA specifically or what, but this Fantasies shit, these people are the real deal, man."

"The real deal? What are you talking about?"

Alan unleashes the kind of exaggerated, movie-like harrumph that indicates far too much time spent in solitude. "What I'm saying, Natalie, my apparently deaf friend, is that these are not the kind of people you want to fuck with."

"Well, if nothing else, I think I can deduce that you have been making some effort to investigate what I asked you to investigate."

"And a fat lot of good it's done me. Do you have any fucking idea how many fucking firewalls, how many fucking traps, how many fucking tricks I've had to dodge just to find my way into their company emails?" He is building up a head of steam again. In shouting, as in sex, he *never* manages that twice. This is bad.

"Well, Alan, I think I'm getting a general impression. What the colloquially inclined might call rather a lot."

"Oh, ha ha ha ha ha ha! Thanks, Natalie, but in the meantime, I'm already one hair trigger away from having the goon squad up my ass and not even close to this top-secret shit you've sent me after. We're talking about a fucking *escort service* here, man. Sure, a major one, a major corporation in fact, but even major corporations, except maybe the Mafia-connected insider trading multinational conglomerate mega-companies, *never* put you through this much trouble just to hack your way to the inner sanctum. The only place you ever see this much security is when you're dealing with the fucking government. And as you know, Natalie, dealing with the government makes me very uncomfortable. That's my first rule, remember? No fucking around with the government unless you're willing to offer a lot more than one blow job."

Natalie sighs, troubled in more ways than she cares to admit. "How many blow jobs do you require now, then? And up front or after the fact?"

"After the fact will be fine, as long as you are willing to guarantee that there will be more than one. And that I won't be going to prison for the rest of my life."

"Now, how the hell can I guarantee that? If what you're saying is true—"

"Okay, I take your point. In that case, I want out."

"Alan, you can't back out now. They're probably already onto you in any case." She strains to sound unconcerned. Her temples want to burst at the seams.

"Yes, they probably are, which is why I fully intend to get the fuck out of this bullshit deal right now unless you can offer me some kind of safety net."

Natalie sighs again, struggling to think past the mounting pain in her head and the mounting itch in her crotch. "Okay, come to think of it, I have a friend in the DA's office. She knows how to make things happen … for the right price."

"Are you sure that you can meet the price?"

"She's my friend. She usually gives discounts for people she likes."

"I can't imagine anyone liking you—even if they were your friend."

"Good point. But if necessary, well, let's just say I know what she enjoys." *If only a word of that was true.*

"What does she like, exactly?" She senses his eyes glittering wet and eager, breathless.

"Trust me, it would be too much for you to handle, little Alan. The secret to getting ahead in this world is to know what people like and give it to them. Personally, I don't often choose to do that, but it makes those times when I do all the more special."

His voice relaxes audibly at the other end, not entirely reassured yet, but no longer throbbing with terror in every breath.

"Well, all right then, if you can guarantee ... if there's at least a chance ... if you think that your friend could ... seriously, you have a friend with the DA's office? You're sure?"

"Yes, dear. Stop being so suspicious. Now, if you'll excuse me, I'm trying to watch the news here and finish a bottle of wine. And I'm sure you'll enjoy the images I've just sent popping through your head a lot more than I will."

With that, she cuts him off, not without some satisfaction. She must have gotten her point across because the phone neither buzzes nor tinkles with the elevator music of a text.

So little Alan likes the idea of fisting. I should remember that.

But she no longer has the energy to dwell upon Alan's strange proclivities. His words come drifting back to her, reaching, as happens sometimes, those parts of herself that she is not sure she wants touched and yet cannot help prodding.

Fantasies Inc. as a heavily fortified branch of the government, of the Secret Service, black ops shit? Son of a bitch. That suspicion was so absurd it was never voiced even in thought, and yet here it is, crawling, skin-inducing …

Oh my word. I knew there was more going on here. I always knew it. I've read about them. With everything I've ever read about them, I knew there was more there. I knew from the moment I set foot in that building, the moment I sat down in front of Erin Hopkins, that fat-assed bitch.

A shudder pulses through her at the thought, she feels her knees curling, muscles contracting. Everything is so right even as it feels so wrong.

Erin, you slippery bitch, what did I ever do to deserve this?

Then the voice on the screen drives all other thoughts from her head.

"Meanwhile, Governor Cole continues to defend her decision not to override the death sentence passed by Judge Hartmann against the Seattle police officers …"

Her colleague Julie Roman has been assigned to cover the case, but Natalie has been following it closely, as has most of the state, much of the country, arguably even much of the rest of the world, for that matter. It has overshadowed her own story, to be honest, more than she would professionally like, still not nearly as much, presumably, as Senator Bergman would prefer.

You see, a couple months ago these three Seattle police officers, Derek Fry, Jon Olsen, Kyle Bolt, all middle-aged white men, were taken into custody after a video went viral, showing them brutally beating, eventually flat-out torturing, and finally killing a homeless black man in a dark Seattle alley in the dead heart of SODO, late at night.

Contrary to what they later claimed, the voices of the officers as heard in the video did not sound inebriated. Nor did the video, which started following the officers while they were cruising the streets, before they even noticed the homeless man, bear out their claim that the man threatened them, claiming that he had a gun (they initially claimed that he pointed a gun at them, but as none was ever found at the scene), nor that he had insulted them with the word "pig" and other "hate slurs."

So, the officers were duly convicted by the jury, and Judge Lucan Hartmann, himself a black man with a long history of activism against police brutality and less of a history of mollification, duly sentenced them all to death by lethal injection, sentence to be carried out in late August, less than a fortnight before the scheduled arms bill vote.

The resulting uproar against the judge's decision from, let's see, the police first and foremost, but also from a lot of other white people, a few black people whose main concern seemed to be the possibility of recriminations from the aforementioned white people, pro-life activists, including the archbishop of Seattle and several other leading clergy of multiple denominations, and a wide variety of similarly concerned persons around the city, state, nation, and globe were all to be expected, along with the several generally anonymous threats made against the life of the judge.

All of which would likely have blown over if Governor Dolores Cole, Democrat, known as a critic of capital punishment and a devout Catholic, also a close friend of Senator Demetrio known to attend Sunday Mass regularly alongside her at Saint James Cathedral, had done as expected and intervened to mitigate the sentence. Instead, she brazenly stood by Judge Hartmann's decision, stating that it was past time the "racist white fascists" were taught a lesson.

When her previous record against the death penalty was called to her attention, Governor Cole pointed out, accurately it was later proven, that she had never claimed to be opposed to capital punishment in all cases, merely in general.

The news shows the wives and children of the three condemned men, three women with seven children between them, standing before a predominantly Caucasian crowd on Pine Street, tears all over their faces, sobbing about how their husbands/daddies are good men, really, who only ever wanted to make the world a better, safer place for all of us, and who, like all men, are nevertheless prone to making mistakes. A reverse shot of the crowd reveals what looks suspiciously like a swastika fluttering from an unreadable banner, way back, almost but not quite off the right edge of the screen.

Cut to Governor Cole's press conference: "I don't care that those men have wives and children. Most of the black men killed every year by racist white fascists, a lot more than three a year, have wives, children, brothers, sisters, mothers, and fathers. Those white children will get by a lot better compared to those black children."

Cut back to CeCe Dahl, her constipated expression matching her constipated voice: "These and other controversial remarks have led to Governor Cole replacing Judge Hartmann as the number one target of death threats."

Natalie has seen enough. Switching off the television, she rolls onto her stomach, turns off the bedside lamp, and lies in darkness, wondering where the hell the world is going, and where she will be when it is done.

In the recesses of her mind, the face of Erin Hopkins swells, leering, in her imagination, the pain mounts in her temples again, the mental image of cement staircases, steel doors, all the Orwellian trappings of the modern-day dungeons of oligarchical dictatorship. Alan's words screaming through her head as painfully and inevitably as fate.

Sometimes, sleep simply will not come, no matter how desperately one cries out for it. Hours blur together

in a muddy trail of agony that seems determined never
to end.

Eventually, she gets up and takes a pill, but the pain
in her temples refuses to recede, as the anticipation
deepens rather, returning to haunt her with the return
of consciousness, she strives to distract herself again,
this time, because it is the first thing that comes to
mind, with the words of Governor Cole, about the
sufferings of the white police officer's children, soon
to be fatherless, juxtaposed with the black children of
the men slain by same.

Is this how black people feel all the time? she wonders,
contemplating the mental image of tangled, scorched
wire that embodies her present predicament, assuming,
as the pessimist in her already does, that Alan's suspicions
concerning Fantasies Inc. are correct, that the nightmare
is only just beginning.

*Is this the bind they find themselves in? How do they
deal with it, if it is? Do they just get used to it? Stop noticing
it? Most of the time? After a while? Am I just getting what I
deserve for being white?*

Somehow—she would not have expected this—it
rather helps to think so.

★   ★   ★

"Senator Bergman. It's a pleasure to meet you.
Though I must admit, it came as a bit of a surprise
when you contacted me."

"It's a pleasure to meet you too, Archbishop. To tell you the truth, I was surprised as well. The power of motherhood, I guess."

"I see. You came to make your mother happy?"

"In a sense, I suppose. She had me baptized as a Catholic, you know, when I was born, though we always attended whatever church my father was orbiting, all the while I was growing up. Anyway, she keeps urging me to go to confession, and then …"

"Time to get the old woman off your back, eh? Well, it happens." Archbishop Luke Bouvier is a short man, albeit burly, the look of an ex–military man about him, in the clipped parting in his gray hair, the firmness behind the kindly, avuncular patience in his elderly face. The tolerance in his voice cannot quite conceal the distaste in his eyes.

"Well, there is that, yes. She sent me a book the other day too, I started flipping through it, and then I read the whole thing in one sitting. It was called *The Fragrance of God* by a woman named Paulette Donahue."

"*Sister* Paulette Donahue. Ah, yes, I'm familiar with that book." Some of the distaste has already faded, replaced by a polite (if still distrustful) interest.

"Whoever she is, yes, she got me to thinking. I particularly admired that passage where she explains the title, where she compares the nature of God to a fragrance, where she talks about how the sense we talk the least about is the olfactory, because it is the most intangible, so we conceive of God most often in visual terms, I suppose for Catholics that's more true than for—other people—but it moved me all the same, the way she analyzed the power of smell, and how it has more to do with the nature of God than any other sense, which in a way is why we think of it the least."

"'As scent is the most ephemeral of the evocative substances, and the most tangential to the thing evoked, so is God in relation to His creation. As one is invaded the most completely and the least intellectually by a fragrance, so one is invaded by God.'" The archbishop plainly knows the book better than indicated.

"Yes, well … that book … it moved me, in a way to which I am not accustomed. And with Bob Dill refusing to answer my calls, with my mother, with everything that is going on …"

He trails off, unsure how to continue, how to explain his presence here in the archbishop's office, in the rectory at Saint James. This is the sort of feeling he hates the most. But the archbishop seems to understand.

"We seek the consolation of religion when the consolations of the world fail us. We should seek God of our own accord, but if that were our first instinct, we would not be men and would have no need to do so."

"Exactly, that's … that's a very, a very helpful way of putting it, Father, I mean, er, Bishop, Archbishop?"

"Just call me Luke. That's quite all right, Senator."

"Very well, thank you. And you may call me Milton, if you like, Luke."

"All right, then, Milton. You said when you contacted me that you wish to undergo the ritual of confession. Do you understand how it works?"

"Well, only from what I've read, what I've seen in movies, you know …"

"Well, there's different ways of doing it. Personally, I prefer to just sit and talk. You tell me whatever you need to unburden. It's best you don't worry about trying to remember everything, every single slip of the tongue, every single lustful thought, what have you. Remember, and this is what I like to tell people, first and foremost: God understands. He understands you better than you, let alone me. You're not here to give the police a report of every detail you can remember from a crime scene, where everything hinges on specifics, specifics, specifics. You are here to unburden your heart, to place yourself in God's infinitely understanding, infinitely loving hands. Does that make sense to you?"

"That sounds … that sounds exactly right, Luke. Thank you."

"Then whenever you're ready, Milton, in your own good time. Take as long as you like. Say whatever you need to say."

How strange to hear those words and not immediately think of the cameras. Though as with any other interview, the first step is the most difficult, and not necessarily what he would have expected.

"When I married my wife … I married my wife, I suppose I loved her, but I knew she was a lesbian. I married her because I needed a wife, for public reasons, and I thought a lesbian would leave me free to philander."

He finally said it. After all these years, he finally said it out loud.

"I see. So you feel that you … lied, in marrying her? That your marriage is a lie? And perhaps that you sinned by intent, by intending to commit adultery, even before you took your wedding vows?"

Someone finally said it. After all these years, he finally heard it said.

"Yes, that's exactly it, Luke. The whole thing was a sham from day one, and it's been a sham ever since. When we … were together, to produce our daughter, it didn't feel like I was forcing her exactly, but that it was another lie, another hypocrisy. Although I love my daughter very much, and so does Vanessa. And then, when it came to other women, well …"

"Yes?" the archbishop urges gently, quiet but forceful, the weight of the public imagination burdening his jaw.

"Well, there have been a lot of them. Not just the Fantasies girl in the hotel a few weeks ago. Oh, yes, I suppose I broke the commandment about lying about that too, on live television. Well, God knows, I'm a politician, it goes without saying that I lie on television, and elsewhere, every day …"

Now the archbishop smiles, for the first time, sincerely. "Even the Bible speaks of the ends justifying the means at times. What is more important to God is what you intended as the ends."

"Yes, well. So, lies without count, sometimes for good ends, I think. I think I had good intentions for them, sometimes. And sometimes not so good. It's hard to say. You get so used to making pragmatic decisions, telling yourself it's for the greater good."

Archbishop Luke is nodding ruefully, lips scrunched together to one side of his mouth. No doubt he knows a thing or two about that himself.

"But getting back to the, uh, the girls, the women, yes, well, there've been, oh, I don't know anymore, maybe two dozen prostitutes, altogether, here and overseas, and that's just what I remember from when I was conscious. There were a few times when I couldn't be quite sure, between the alcohol and the cocaine." *Christ, I hope there are no microphones in this office.* "I mean, I can't pretend I thought that was for the greater good, except my own, right at that moment."

"If we are a moment of God's time, what is a moment of our own to God?"

That one stumps Milton for a minute. Not only the words, but what Luke was trying to tell him with them.

"Well, all I know is, all it takes is a moment to ruin an entire life, an entire career, a lot of things. I guess that's why I lie so much. Anyway, like I say, there were a good two dozen prostitutes, maybe more, and then there were the women I didn't pay. How many? God, I don't know how many, not as many. A lot of secretaries, just a couple of colleagues, rich women, donor types." Another, far guiltier memory swims to the surface, making him flush, surprising that he has not remembered it before now, that all these other things seemed to take precedence.

Luke notices the flush. "Is that all?" As politely, forgivingly inquiring as God asking Adam why he betrayed him.

Milton sighs. What the hell. Literally. "Okay, well, there was, there is, this other girl, she was fifteen." *Oh, Christ, how I hope there are no microphones in this office.* "She was fifteen when we met, and she's my daughter's best friend." The words are making him feel filthier than he has ever felt. It never felt this way, not even when they were in bed together, not when he thought about it even in his most recalcitrant moments. Why is he filled with shame, the reality of his criminal status now? "Actually, no, she was much younger. We *met* her practically when she was born. She was a beautiful child. It was my daughter's sixteenth birthday, and she was still fifteen. That was the day we first …"

He can no more.

"And, from what you said, it sounds like you've *known* her since?"

"Yes, many times. My daughter knows—she walked in on us the first time." A sick urge to laugh swells up in his stomach at the thought. "I think she's the only one who knows. Well, not quite, my wife may know, my aides may know, but none of them care. My daughter is the only one who cares, and she cares too much about both of us, well, about her friend, anyway, to say anything." Is he confessing now or reassuring himself?

The archbishop is still nodding, as tolerant as ever. For the first time, the link dawns on Bergman between the nature of the sin he has just confessed and the denomination of the clergy he has confessed it to.

"Do you intend to put an end to this affair?" Archbishop Luke inquires, rather more sharply. The question takes Bergman by surprise.

"You know, I never thought about it. She's grown up now. It's not illegal."

"It is still adultery."

Ouch.

"Of course it is. And, yes, I suppose it's hypocritical to confess it if I have no intention of stopping. That makes sense. To tell you the truth, every time we do it, I always think it will be the last time. And it gets closer and closer to being the truth."

"Why is that?"

Bergman looks up at him and sees the honest perplexity there, the battling suspicions, seeking to make truth out of the cryptic wording, the various impressions gleaned from the news. And finally he wants to tell him, to tell him what this is really all about, what really drove him here, what moved him so deeply about the book his mother sent him, what drove him to accede to his mother's conscientious requests at last, what drove him to discard caring about the preservation of a public image twenty years in the building.

"I have cancer, Luke."

The archbishop is silent for quite a while. "I see," he says finally, folding his hands under his chin.

Now that he has let it out, all Bergman wants to do is shut it up again. Another question is sorely troubling him in any case. "Archbishop, I mean, Luke, can I ask you, is it a sin, do you think, to desire a teenage girl? I mean, I know, of course, the way the rules are written, you're not supposed to entertain the thoughts and everything, which, forgive me, we all know is kind of bullshit, but I mean, there was a time when it was legal, a moment of God's time as it were. Hell, in a lot of places, it still is. You know, age of consent has always been a work in progress. But what I mean is, I know it was wrong of me, in many ways, but, I guess, how wrong? What was the sin, exactly?"

The clergyman stares at him long and hard, visibly pondering the question. "The thing about sexual relations with a minor—the thing about sexual relations with anyone, for that matter—is that sex has the power to hurt people. Permanently. Irrevocably. If you disregard that, then you are in a state of sin." His voice is firm, on the verge of anger, but there is moderation in his tone as well as he goes on. "I sometimes find myself telling people—this may not be strictly orthodox, but it is my personal interpretation—that it is not so much that adultery, fornication, that extramarital or premarital sexual relations are wrong in and of themselves. It is more that they have enormous power to disrupt other people's lives in ways that we cannot predict, and which we disregard at our own, but what is infinitely worse, at other's peril. Obviously, sexuality is an enormously irrepressible part of our buildups, and we cannot always repress it without causing similar imperilment, and sometimes, that inability must coincide with an inability to find sexual fulfillment with a spouse. And of course, there are times when married sex has the power to hurt, to disrupt, to damage either or both parties, and parties beyond. This is what we are supposed to think of, what God wants us to think of, in all that we do."

The archbishop sighs again, looks into the increasingly sad-hound eyes of the senator, and continues more gently. "As for whether it is always wrong to lust after a teenage girl, or anyone else, well, I agree, the body wants what the body wants. Desire is not sinful in and of itself. Sin lies with intent; that is the core teaching on the subject, at least in Catholic theology. God gives the gift of beauty because He wants it to be appreciated. And, of course, there are few things more beautiful than a beautiful young person. I was speaking once to a young man who had been seduced by his parish priest, thankfully not in my diocese, as a sixteen-year-old. They formed a relationship that lasted for six months—and ended when the priest in question was arrested. This boy was heartbroken; he did not perceive the priest as an abuser at all. I could not believe my ears, and of course, it did not change the fact that the priest was both a sinner and a criminal, unfit for his office in every sense, but this boy, well, I did not know what to say to him. It was possibly the strangest conversation of my life, and it was more than a little disturbing. He kept saying to me that this priest was a good man, an aesthete, who had merely seen in him what the ancient Greeks saw in young men at the height of civilization and acted accordingly." The archbishop snorts and shakes his head. "I think he must have read that in a book somewhere; nothing else he said was remotely so articulate. Anyway, I fancy he felt much the same way as your daughter's friend feels toward yourself. If that helps at all."

Bergman is not certain whether it helps or not, but he feels better than he did before. The confession continues for a while, and when it is over, after the archbishop has lain a soft hand on the senator's head and mumbled the words of absolution, after he has gifted Bergman with a rosary on which to say his penance, when he walks down the steps from the office to the front door of the rectory and exits, finding himself in the brilliant sunlight beneath the golden pink of Japanese cherry blossoms that emit a fragrance truly divine, he cannot help feeling that he has wasted his life after all.

★   ★   ★

Speaking of wasted lives, Alan has never given much thought to what a successful life would be.

All for the best. The prospect would surely make him even more depressed than usual, which would be quite an accomplishment.

The world has weighed heavily on his back for as long as he can remember. Perhaps somewhere way back, all the way back to the earliest vestiges of selfhood, a toddler maybe, too early to have had enemies, to have been worthy of notice. Nothing but mother's love, mother's milk, mother's breasts, when that was his entire world, then he may have been happy. Who can say?

An empty bag of Cheetos slips from between his orange-dusted fingers, orange imprints where his fingertips have made contact with the laptop keys.

The eyes are back. That much he can remember from earliest childhood quite distinctly: the sense of being watched. Watched by whom, he has never been certain. He was not raised to be religious, so that rules out the demons of hell. For all he knows, it could be the angels of the paradise he does not believe in. They would probably have as much reason to be angry with him as everyone else—everything else in his world.

It occurs to him, not for the first time, that the root of his troubles may be not the eyes but his sincere curiosity concerning their origin. They do not disturb him as much as it seems they should. He almost wishes sometimes that they would come out of the gadget-laden shadows to keep him company. They might be succubi. That would liven things up, whether they were evil or not. They could not possibly be worse than relying on that scrawny journalist for companionship.

He has experienced sleep paralysis more than once in his life. Watching *Nightmare on Elm Street* the first time was like experiencing a documentary, but even the penetrating glare of paranoia-conjured ice-cold demonic energy never frightened him the way it should have, not the way it troubles those whimpering fools on the support group websites with their endless talk of shadow men and damnation.

If only he could believe that it was some proof of life beyond these walls, beneath this stinking floor, these bare walls, this barren technology. Even if that proof were evil, at least there would be more after all. Some chance of existence after the men in black come bursting through the door, through the windows, out from behind the plaster, up from beneath the mountains of trash in every corner, leeching out of his reeking hovel to carry him away to some fate that cannot possibly be worse than this.

It could not possibly be worse, and that frightens him nevertheless. It frightens him worse than the eyes, makes the feeble horror of merely being watched a mockery, frightens him the way death must frighten the trembling creatures at the zoo, the ones that cannot mate in captivity, the ones who have nothing left to live for, the ones who have nothing to look forward to but fear and pain and yet tremble at the prospect of worse.

For it can always get worse. This he has learned, every single day of his life, as far as he can remember. A progression from worse to worse, such has been the progression of his days, greater pain mounting upon him every single day, the mounting ache in his genitals, somehow not slaked but rather exacerbated by his infrequent humping sessions with the Schroder woman whenever she needs him.

To think he could not lose his virginity until he met that woman—not that he ever expected his first time to be with a supermodel or even one of the prettier girls he had the misfortune to encounter in all his miserable years at school. To think that she is probably the only woman he will ever have had sex with when he goes to his grave, even if that day be far away, fifty years away, though he is certain it will not be that long, panic tells him he probably has less than fifty days, fifty hours or less in fact, nothing but a web of pain, more excruciating than anything imaginable, for the depth of his transgression. Yes, he can sense it coming: agony beyond comprehending at the hands of the monstrous powers his meddling fingers have disturbed.

Alan can sense the headache pending even as he fades into a troubled sleep.

★　★　★

The parking is always a nightmare along the waterfront, any hour of any day of the week. That's why Natalie takes a cab to and from the office the day after receiving the coded note.

She asks the turbaned driver to stay where he is, let the meter run until she gets back, and heads into Boris's Tavern, a sizable establishment carefully crafted to evoke a New England hole in the wall, despite having clearly been recently renovated.

Nevertheless, the interior appeals oddly to Natalie's taste: clean, polished oak and other dark wood panels everywhere, elegant maritime paintings, artificial portholes sometimes functioning as windows and sometimes not. A cheerful atmosphere accompanies the scents of cooking oil, fish, steak, french fries, and, of course, alcohol.

Since she has no clue what Philip Golding will look like, she takes a seat at the bar, counting on her precisely chosen red suit jacket and intellectually cropped hair to convey her identity to him when he is ready to appear.

Natalie is by no means certain whether it is a good idea to have alcohol in her veins for a meeting like this, but when a burly man whose dress shirt and tie clashes sharply with his whiskered, naturally glowering features takes a seat on the stool next to her and asks if she has ever before met a man who can speak three languages at the same time, she has little choice but to order the sangria for which she is dying.

The man has spouted several mangled phrases comprised of what is clearly intended to be French and what is less clearly intended to be two other languages, while Natalie has downed two glasses of sangria in five minutes and is working on a third, when she feels the expected—and merciful—tug on her left elbow.

"Ms. Schroder, if you would accompany to my table in the corner," says a young man with spiky pink hair and lips like a Latina porn star.

He doesn't sound gay. "Gladly." She hauls herself off the stool while the contractor, apparently unaware, mumbles what sounds like "Guillermo, Guillermo, Guillermo" in a loop that may never end.

The corner to which the young man in leather leads her is cool and shadowed, a single bulb concealed behind red glass hanging over the square table.

"If you wouldn't mind handing me your phone," the boy says, pulling out Natalie's chair for her and holding out his disconcertingly soft hand.

"Okay," she mutters, slightly perplexed, handing it over and watching as he deposits it in a small black box that disappears into one of his coat pockets before he takes his seat opposite her.

"I want to make sure our conversation isn't recorded," he says by way of explanation as he sits down and takes up his glass of gin. "I know how to protect my devices, but it would take too long to reprogram yours right now."

"I understand completely," she says, truthfully, sipping sangria without taking her gray eyes off his blue ones.

He seems in no hurry to get to the point. Their conversation meanders through a long series of formulaic platitudes, during which they both have their drinks refilled more than once.

When a group of loud men takes a seat at the table immediately to Natalie's right, Philip's manner abruptly changes. Leaning across the table, he whispers, "Now that we can talk without being overheard? What do you want to know, Miss Schroder? I'm not sure if I'll be able to help you or not. All Billy told me was that I needed to meet you, that I might be able to help you. He and I don't always know the same things, so ..."

He leaves the implication hanging. Natalie conceals her annoyance at the realization that this young man is probably going to be just as useless as the all the rest. "I am looking for the girl who was involved with Senator Milton Bergman at the Seashell Hotel. And any other information about Fantasies Inc. that you can give me. Anything to do with the Reich controversy. Anything and everything."

The young man nods, slowly, understandingly, remaining bent in his halfway-across-the-table posture. "I figured it would be something like that." He sits back slowly and regards her with his fingers steepled under his chin, lightly frowning.

Natalie is starting to get a headache. *Endless small talk is bad enough without theatrics.*

The boy finally shifts his chair closer to her, around the edge of the table, and beckons for her to do the same.

Bending his face to within a few inches of her left ear, he mutters, "I can't lead you to the girl, but I can tell you who she isn't, if that helps. And there are things I can tell you about … those other things you mentioned. Not much, but some."

"If you don't mind me asking, first, who *are* you, exactly?"

"Twombly gave you my name, I'm sure. I used to work directly under him. I was his personal assistant. Now I'm the assistant to his replacement's assistant. Demotion, I suppose, although they pay me the same. They don't trust me as much as they did before—nor should they." He chuckles mirthlessly, a sound too old for his young face, and continues. "A couple years ago, you see, my good old boss, Billy, he starts to notice some strange numbers cropping up in the system. Big-dollar numbers that don't quite line up with our records. So, he goes to the big boss, Darryl Eaton, or he tries to, anyway. Mr. Eaton's a hard man to get a grasp on, doesn't spend much time at the office. Of course, it's a big company, but most of the time, he never seems to be quite anywhere. Very strange. But you can always get ahold of him by phone. At least in theory. Turns out to be theory whenever Billy tries to contact him about these numbers.

"So, you know, a month or two goes by like this, and Billy's getting more and more suspicious, and he's also getting suspicious about some of his employees, especially this young buck named Vincent Chow. Puts in weird hours, doesn't show up for meetings, always has a really good excuse, and gets his work done with almost inhuman speed and efficiency when he actually sits down to do it. It all makes Mr. Twombly increasingly nervous. So, eventually, he decides he can't take it anymore. He's sick of being ignored by his superiors about this obvious incongruence and having to worry about this untrustworthy employee, he whips out the old cheat book and hacks into Vincent's computer. And lo and behold, what do you think he finds, plain as day, sitting right there for all the hacker world to see?" He interrupts himself to take a sip of gin.

Natalie waits impatiently for him to go on, but he seems to be expecting her to ask. At length, she gives in. "So, what does he find?"

He effects a pained expression. "Well, that's the thing, you see. I never quite found out. I don't think he wants me to know too much—for my own safety. Probably wise. I'm not sure how bad I want to know, to tell you the truth. What I do know is—whatever he found, it scared the living shit out of him. Pissed him off too. Which is a very unfortunate combination, as it turns out. Impotent rage. Not fun.

"Like I say, he never tells me exactly what he found, but he starts muttering to himself all the time, where I can hear, muttering about how we're working for a bunch of crooks, a bunch of cyber-criminals, a bunch of liars, corruption, you name it. Starts getting bags under his eyes, starts drinking. Sad sight. Still a great boss, but in bad shape. Needed help, couldn't get it from that bitch wife of his." He finishes the last of his gin and gasps heavily. "Time goes by, things seem to settle down a bit, boss is still in bad shape, but he's getting used to it, I'm getting used to his muttering, things are bad, but it seems like they might just get better. Eventually, somehow. Then, out of the blue, along comes this reporter, guy named Ben Corker. Real fireball. He starts coming into the office, asking Billy all sorts of questions, off the record, 'an anonymous insider at Eaton's says you know,' that sort of thing, all very deliberately vague, but Billy was happy to talk to him. And he had a lot to tell him. I never heard most of it, but what I did hear, it was … illuminating."

A brunette waitress in a wench's uniform that exposes a considerable amount of her not-so-considerable bosom approaches to refill their drinks. Philip and Natalie study her with identical expressions as she leans forward with her pitchers.

When she has gone, Philip sips deeply and sighs, not with satisfaction but with some sort of pain. Whether from the burning gin or his memories, Natalie cannot tell.

"The bigwigs were in league with Giulio Visconti," he says bluntly, and not very quietly, all the more unfortunate as the group at the opposite table has finally reached a lull. He continues more discreetly, "That was the one thing he knew for sure. That was where the unaccountable millions came from."

Natalie nods, taking a sip of sangria so deep her ears turn to flame. This is where she has sensed the conversation going, drawing ever closer to the quivering, perilous heart of the spider's web.

"What it was all for, what we were giving them in return, I never found out. The only thing I never knew for sure was this: Visconti had a girl whose market value he wanted us to appraise. That was probably what Chow was working on, that upset Billy so much. The girl's name was Claudia Mortmain, or so Visconti claimed." The boy reaches into his pocket and pulls out the largest iPhone Natalie has ever seen, just a hair too small to be a tablet. The image he intends to show her is right there when he switches it on, carefully angled under the tabletop.

Natalie finds herself looking into the eyes of a girl of indeterminate age and ethnicity, obviously quite young and rather dark-skinned, but otherwise indecipherable. The photo shows her from the waist up, naked, yet aside from her face, it would be difficult to tell that she was a girl.

"Of course, you know that Visconti was brought to book for trafficking in underage girls—and the equally terrible crime of gambling." Philip snorts with contemptuous laughter. "Why it was so important for Chow to assess her value, her value to whom, how exactly he was going about the job, I don't know. You'd think Fantasies Inc. could take care of that on their own. If they were crazy enough to deal with underage girls in the first place. Nothing would surprise me, of course. Whatever. I'll never know the details. All I know is, after Corker got arrested, Billy comes to me and gives me this picture to hold onto, and another photo that I am going to show you in a moment. He also gives me some other things of no direct interest to you, tells me to hang onto them against the day of judgment as he put it, and then he retires to California with a pension from the company bigger than Mount Rainier."

"You think he actually managed to blackmail those people? That seems almost unbelievable … just because I can't imagine anyone being able to beat them."

"You've got the right idea there. Of course, Billy didn't exactly beat them. It was more of a draw, the way I see it. He gets to spend the rest of his life looking over his shoulder, hoping they don't decide to hedge their bets and just cut their losses by getting him out of the way. *All the way* out of the way."

More than the sangria is sinking in Natalie's stomach as she contemplates those words. From the look on his face, the same is true for Philip.

"You said ... you said there was another photograph?"

"Yes." Philip swipes his thumb to the left and a second image appears, much darker, a horizontal image for which he has to turn the phone on its side to maximize the viewing experience. Even so, the image is murky, almost indiscernible. Four figures standing in front of a nondescript wall, perhaps at twilight, filmed through a telephoto lens undoubtedly. At the left, she eventually recognizes the distinctive outline of former Governor Jules Reich, face turned to his left, toward the other three. To his immediate right, a shape that forms itself, with some help from the imagination, into Giulio Visconti, and to his right, a shape whose blockish head and height point to the elusive Jupiter Strong, features entirely hidden in shadow. The same is to be said for the figure at the far right, whose figure seems somewhat curvier and shorter than the other three, implying a woman. That's all Natalie can tell.

She says as much to Philip. He nods affirmatively.

"That's exactly what I made of it. Who the woman might be, I could not say. Not that names mean very much when you're dealing with that lot anyway."

"What do you mean, exactly?" There's that chill again, eating away at her spine.

"Well, you know what they say about Larsen's Reproductions. They can turn you into literally anything. The only thing they can't directly do anything about is your height and all that. And as for Fantasies, well, one does hear the strangest rumors. One scarcely knows what to believe, but it goes without saying that they specialize in secrecy, which is not an easy thing to do in a corporation that size. Makes you think they must know how to do things, things you and I wouldn't think of, or if we did think of them, would never credit, we'd tell ourselves we were being paranoid because we didn't want to think anything so horrible could be true."

The ball of poison in Natalie's stomach is leeching out into the rest of her system, filling her body with icy heat. Her fingertips are trembling again. "So … what exactly are you implying?" She spills an ounce of sangria.

"I don't know, to tell you the truth. All I know is I've tried to get a grasp on that organization, and trying to catch fog doesn't begin to describe it."

Natalie knows a thing or two about that. She is about to ask for her phone back—there is definitely a note of finality in Philip's manner—when one last question occurs to her. "I don't suppose you know for sure, but … what happened to that girl?"

He only looks puzzled for a second. "Who … oh, Claudia? Oh, well, it's funny you should ask. Right after Reich resigned, right before Corker was arrested, I caught sight of an ad in my junk mail, advertising this book, this tell-all book, with a face on the cover that looked suspiciously like Miss Mortmain's. Didn't catch the name of the author. The image was too small. I clicked on it, and my computer got a virus. Go figure. That's the last I ever saw of her or that book. I can't remember what the title was supposed to be. I never found it again. I looked."

"I suppose they may have let her go, if they knew she could hurt them ... rather like with your boss."

"Exactly like with Billy, as a matter of fact."

He suddenly looks smug. She recalls his remark from earlier, that he could tell her decisively who the girl at the hotel wasn't.

"What else do you know about her?" Her voice conveys that she is not in the mood for beating around the bush.

He leans in conspiratorially and whispers, "Look to your left."

From where she is sitting, Natalie's face is exactly level with one of the porthole windows, situated approximately three feet from her chair. The bar-restaurant resides on a quay, but there is an entire parking lot squeezed onto the quay, separating it from the fence that protects pedestrians from the waters of Puget Sound.

At first, she cannot make out anything much through the dark, but at length, she discerns, limned against the light from one of the structures on the pier to the south, the shape of a girl, leaning against the fence, gazing down into the water.

"Twombly managed to protect her by getting her information when he hacked Chow," Philip confides. "She and I have been in contact ever since. She won't tell me what the deal was with that book—maybe she doesn't even know. Billy's not the only hacker in the world. It put her in danger for a while. Like I said, when you're in a stalemate, you don't want to upset the balance. But she got through it somehow, and it eventually blew over. Now all she does is keep her head down. I check up on her periodically, make sure everything's okay. Part of her security."

"So, can you?"

He slides a card with an address into her hand and stands up. "I'm afraid I can't tell you anything more, Miss Schroder. I hope I have been of assistance to you." He reaches into his pocket and takes her phone out of the black case. "It's been a pleasure to meet you!" He leans in unexpectedly, kisses her on the forehead, and then disappears into the crowded space.

By the time Natalie turns to look out the window, the shadowed girl has vanished as well.

CHAPTER SEVEN

The address on the card leads Natalie to an apartment building in north Seattle, up where the suburbs are fading into Shoreline, where the gray of the Sound seems to have filtered into the landscape, into the houses and trees and everything else.

On the back of the card, Philip had scribbled the suggestion that Natalie wait a few days before seeking the girl out. She has decided to heed his advice.

More perplexing is the remaining question of why Philip did not find it necessary to include a phone number or email address on the paper, or at least a suggestion of when it might be most convenient for her to meet Claudia. The first two options at least have their obvious drawbacks.

So, she drives up there at her own convenience, hoping to all the gods she can't believe in that the girl will be home when she gets there.

She need not have worried, as it turns out. That is to say, she need not have worried about the possibility that the girl would not be home.

The apartment building is nearly as depressing an affair as the Corkers' dwelling, though it has the redeeming grace of being a quaint building in an older sort of neighborhood, one of those increasingly few places where all the houses look different because they were not all built by the same contractor. Claudia's apartment is the second from the southmost, on the upper floor, reached by a rickety staircase that feels as though it is going to collapse even under Natalie's meager weight.

The girl called Claudia opens the door almost at the first knock, as though she had been expecting company. Natalie supposes that Philip may have warned her, but that possibility seems at odds with the fear, surprise, and apprehension in the girl's eyes, not unlike the expression she wore in the picture. Natalie has the strange impression that the girl is in the habit of lurking near the door, perhaps to ambush anyone she considers suspicious.

"Good afternoon," Natalie says gently, nervously, sensing that speaking too loudly would make the girl wince with fear. "Are you, um, Claudia Mortmain?"

The girl stares at her, lips trembling, eyes focused, not confused, definitely comprehending, yet hesitant, undecided. Natalie intuits that nothing she can do or say is going to affect that reticence.

After a pause during which Natalie can hear her own heartbeat distinctly, or maybe it is the girl's, a whispered response finally comes. "Yes. That's ... me."

There is a trace of an accent in the voice, but the girl speaks so quietly that she cannot tell where it might be from any more than she can deduce the girl's ethnicity.

The silence lengthens and lengthens until Natalie knows she is going to be doing far more of the talking here. "May I, ahem, may I come in?" she mutters, attempting to speak up but still anxious about upsetting the girl. Her voice ends on a squeaking note that she would despise in anyone's voice.

But the edge of firmness seems to have injected the faintest fiber of decisiveness in the girl. She looks left and right and then says, "Okay, yes, come in."

Natalie follows the girl into a squalid living room containing only a colorless couch, a lawn table, and an ageless pole lamp. Gray drapes flutter over a half-open window, looking out on a grove of fir trees. Natalie is surprised this girl would leave her drapes undrawn, much less over an open window.

In the light of the living room, Natalie is finally able to get a decent look at the girl. She wears what was once a green tank top and a pair of men's boxers, with a turquoise sandal on her left foot and nothing on the right. She is prettier in person than in the picture, a fact that is somehow emphasized rather than diminished by her fear.

"Shall we ... take a seat?" Natalie asks.

The girl looks at her, then at the couch, and gives a small nod. "Sure."

Natalie takes a seat with an alarming creaking of springs, but the girl remains standing, first staring at her guest and then ambling aimlessly toward the window.

"Ms. Mortmain, I need to talk to you about your experience with an organization known as Fantasies Incorporated. Would you be willing to talk to me about that?"

The girl does not look at her or change her expression while Natalie is speaking, but after the words have trailed into silence, she slowly turns her head, eyes narrowing, lips trembling again, tilting her face to the left as though questioning the question.

Natalie is on the verge of repeating herself when the girl finally says, "What do you want?" Her voice is loud, sharp, approaching anger, completely at odds with what has preceded it.

Unsure whether she is making progress but grateful that the whispering is over, Natalie says, "I want to know about Fantasies Incorporated, the company that Giulio Visconti sold you to. I want to know about you, about your experience."

The girl blinks, trembles, turns her face back toward the window. A stab of pity pierces Natalie's heart. She hates to contemplate lives such as this girl's. There is nothing more awful than hopelessness—in oneself or in others—yet the pity does not make it any easier to sympathize with the girl's vacantness.

Natalie leans forward, striving to make her voice sound soothing. "Where are you from, Claudia? Where were you born?"

Once again, the girl seems not to have heard. Some thought is pressing at the edge of Natalie's mind, some contradiction that will elude her until it is too late.

A gentle breeze ruffles the girl's hair, sending a long black strand curling under her nose and over her lips. She reaches up and brushes it away immediately. A spike of disgust is rallying to plunge itself through Natalie's forehead.

There is an orange bottle of pills on the table, quite empty. Natalie is surprised she didn't notice it until now. A hint of fear clouds her features as well.

Natalie is halfway across the room when the girl starts to tremble all over. She is reaching a hand toward Claudia's shoulder when the girl spins around, eyes looking not at her guest or at the wall but somewhere beyond, brown eyes full of pain.

The girl seems to panic when she notices Natalie's outstretched arm, but it is a silent panic, one that consists entirely of swiping feebly at the extended hand.

Natalie retracts the hand, but the girl keeps swiping at the air, lips trembling, a whimper building in her throat, eyes blinking rapidly.

"Are you okay?" Natalie asks clearly and concisely, already knowing the answer.

The girl shakes and shakes, backing away now, backing toward the window, cringing, whining, shaking her head, burying her face in her hands. Her breathing seems to be growing deeper, approaching hyperventilation.

Within a matter of minutes, the girl is curled up beneath the window, muttering uncontrollably, every muscle in her body twitching. Upon closer inspection, Natalie detects the flecks of foam at the edges of her mouth.

When the ambulance arrives, they find Natalie on her knees with her arms around the unconscious girl, stroking her dark hair with shaking hands. When they draw nearer, they see that the journalist's cheeks are streaked with tears.

Hours later, at the hospital, the doctor informs Natalie that the girl overdosed on some sleeping pill she has never heard of. She is in a coma now, responding well to treatment, but there is no telling when she will wake up.

Natalie collapses on her way through the parking lot. When the orderlies have carried her back into the hospital, she is diagnosed with extreme stress-induced fatigue and compelled to spend the night.

Sometime in the middle of the night, Natalie wakes up with an idea fully formed in her head, as though her sleeping mind had been cogitating on it all night.

That night at Boris's Tavern, she had looked out the window and seen a girl, a girl whom Philip claimed was Claudia.

The Claudia she had met did not seem like she could have gone outside even before she entered her coma. And come to think of it, if Philip had been aware of her incapacity, well, that could explain his perplexing failure to arrange a specific meeting.

The dark hospital ceiling soon smothers Natalie into a nightmare-laden sleep.

Senator Bergman Condemns Execution of "SODO 3"

by Natalie Schroder
June 15, 20—

SEATTLE—In a press conference Thursday, Senator Milton Bergman (R-WA) criticized the decision by Governor Dolores Cole not to override the judgment passed by Judge Hartmann against the three police officers convicted of brutally torturing and killing a Seattle homeless man of African American ethnicity.

"We cannot prevent evil by doing evil, and a stated opponent of capital punishment is a hypocrite if ever they forget that," said Bergman.

This was the senator's first public comment on the subject, as well as his first public appearance of any sort since the KOMO 4 panel last week. The comment was much in keeping with current Republican attitudes toward Judge Hartmann's sentence.

Bergman, however, seemed to be deliberately distancing himself from the established right-wing position when he went on to say that the three officers should, while being allowed to live, serve a lengthy prison sentence and be removed from the force.

"There is no place for men like that on the police force," Bergman stated emphatically, going on to imply an intention to use his office to address police brutality.

While these remarks would appear to have driven a wedge between Bergman and Seattle Chief of Police Grace Howitzer, one of the few women to support him in the wake of the recent hotel scandal, the statement has appeal for some Seattle voters.

"This was a very brave statement for the senator to make," commented Roxane Keen, an African American anti-police brutality advocate who has taken a similar stance toward the so-called SODO 3. "For a white Republican male US senator to recommend the discharge and imprisonment of white police officers in a crime of this magnitude, this has never been done before. He knows what effect that could have in his constituency."

Senator Bergman's core of support does not seem to have been much affected by the news, however, perhaps because they, like many Democrats and other critics, have interpreted the press conference as an attempt by the senator to distract attention away from his other troubles.

"This is nothing more than a transparently obvious attempt to deflect the media toward an equally controversial issue, tempered by a moderate stance, and away from his recent disgrace," stated Senator Chloe Demetrio (D–WA) who has refused to take a strong stance on the subject but who has offered some muted words of support for her friend Governor Cole.

"This is a case of conscience," Demetrio went on to say, "and Cole and Hartmann have at least listened to theirs. Bergman, as far as I can tell, is simply exploiting the situation to redeem his own public image. I can think of nothing more despicable."

★   ★   ★

That's all Natalie has been able to write about Bergman in the last week, and it is making her situation at the office ever more untenable.

Twice already, she has been called into Karin's office to deliver an update on the assignment, to account for her low output, for her mounting liability to the organization, for her ugly face and her bad attitude, for ever being born.

Karin can no longer be troubled to call her in on the landline or by email. No, she has to send Marla's fat ass sauntering all the way down to Natalie's cubicle, swaggering with those officiously graceful steps that just happen to set everything a-jiggling, all to announce in that bright perky voice, "Good morning, Natalie!

Say, if you have a minute, Karin really wants to see you in her office!"

Exact same wording, both times. Carbon copies. Rather like her buttocks and her tits. At least she got to admire those in full, all the way to Karin's office. *Cunt.*

The first time, she was at least able to play on her hospitalization. Even Karin could not think of a way to scold her for that. The second time, Natalie walked out while her boss was in the middle of a tirade on accountability that might have done a frizzy third grade teacher proud.

In the meantime, she has pored over every inch of Corker's notes and come up with nothing new. The incomplete names are worthless in an online search—not that she hasn't tried. She has been looking over every one of Corker's articles and every other article she can find relating to Fantasies Inc., to Larsen's, to the Governor Reich affair, everything that Cynthia Heiner published on the subject, looking for any connection, anything she has not noticed before, and found nothing.

After storming out of her second meeting with Karin, she flung herself down behind her desk and, in a moment of fevered clarity, found herself ruminating again on the question of Philip Golding and the mysterious figure he had claimed was Claudia Mortmain. Was it possible that he had coaxed the girl out of her isolation somehow, that what she had witnessed at the girl's apartment was an anomaly?

No. The girl had obviously been a wreck far longer than that. Who could blame her, considering what she had been

*through … whatever that may have been. No, Golding must
have gotten some girl—hell, considering his own appearance,
maybe not even a girl—to play the part on the quayside that
night, in order to tantalize me.*

She thought about trying to contact him, but soon
thought better of it. To think that he had tricked her …
simply to tantalize her, to get her to go to Claudia's
apartment? The more she thought about it, the more
perplexing it becomes. *If he's not really working for
Twombly … or can I even be certain of Twombly?*

The mental image of the girl's image on the cover
of a tell-all book rises, along with a taste curiously like
sulfur.

*How can you hope to be certain of anything, of anyone,
when you're dealing with organizations that specialize in
reconstruction, brainwashing, mind-altering substances no
doubt? How else do they get their employees to do what they
ask, to be so perfectly secretive, so discreet, so compliant? Oh
my sweet little baby Jesus.*

The only name in Corker's notes that generated
any semblance of an external link was an Adrienne U
(=*EH?*). Upon inspection, Natalie found references to
a book titled *A Look Back on Being Hooked* by Adrienne
Urquhart, who claimed to be have been used as a girl by
the architects of Project MKUltra back in the fifties and
sixties, forced to perform oral sex on a group of CIA
agents as a way to guarantee their complicity in illegally
dosing unwilling participants with LSD and Christ
knows what else. The book was made unavailable when
a wide range of inconsistencies made it susceptible

to libel charges, most notably the fact that Urquhart was revealed not to have been born until almost after MKUltra was discontinued.

The initials *EH* continue to trouble her with their disconcerting familiarity until Marla goes bustling past her cubicle, fortunately without speaking to her for once, and the thought of Erin Hopkins arises in Natalie's mind again.

Adrienne Urquhart = Erin Hopkins?

How could Urquhart and Hopkins be the same person? For that matter, *why* would they be? Unless, of course, one thought of long-lost Project MKUltra as a stand-in for Fantasies Inc. and its practices, if it was an allegory, and that was why …

Of course, Corker was only speculating. How could Hopkins still be employed as a top executive of Fantasies if she had tried to write a tell-all? That would make no sense. She would have ended up like poor Claudia.

Unless, that is, the Hopkins she had met was not the real Hopkins, if she was someone else, if her name was as much as mask as a Larsen's face-lift, as that body, which had struck her as a work of Larsen's art.

And if a mind can be retouched as easily as a body.

Her aching mind floats across the other equations in Corker's pages, linking Jupiter Strong, Giulio Visconti, Governor Reich, and Darryl Eaton to so many other obscure initials, half ideas. *Suppose all their names were nothing but masks.*

When the memory of that second picture from Philip's phone crosses her mind, when she remembers that feminine figure at the right edge of the image, when it finally dawns on her that said figure is most likely the elusive *EH*, the initials most used alongside the other, more recognizable initials that link so easily with the more easily recognized figures in the picture, Natalie feels as though she has been stabbed in the stomach. Too late, she realizes she is going to be sick.

She stumbles out of the cubicle, and when Marla whirls around and asks in that brightly inquisitive voice if Natalie is all right, the gorge rises irrepressibly in her throat—and she throws up all over that elegant gray blouse and black skirt.

★ ★ ★

Eight days after their last conversation, Natalie's phone buzzes with the name of Alan shining bright. She is still in the middle of her evening wine, her third glass that is, sitting at the table before the remnants of a rotisserie chicken and the remnants of Corker's notes, Sapphire curled at her feet.

"Hello?"

"Hey, Natalie, it's me."

"Wait, what? How did you get this number?"

"Oh, please, Natalie. I'm not in the mood."

"Oh, you're never in the mood anymore, you heartless bastard."

She can feel his mouth twitching in spite of his face all the way through the phone. "Listen, Nat, I'm sorry it's been taking so long, but I think I've made a break."

The haze of red fumes has made her faintly lightheaded, but she sits up straight. "That's great. What have you found? Why did it take so long?"

"You're a grateful one, aren't you? It took so long because, even aside from dodging a veritable mountain of security, the Fantasies files are the most convoluted, confusing, jumbled mass of shit you'll find outside of a sewage treatment pond. You wouldn't believe some of the shit they've got in their system. And when it comes to finding a specific employee, well, Christ, I knew they were in a very cooperative relationship with Larsen's, but I never knew how much they relied on them. There are some girls, even a few men working for them who've had their whole bodies altered six times in the past six months. And for every single one of those alterations, a dozen pages of web to sift through, with specifications, the details, the fantasy they're working to build, everything has to be just right. It's unbelievable."

Even Natalie is mildly taken aback. "Six times in six months, whole new faces, whole new everything? That's incredible. I didn't even know Larsen's—"

"So, when it comes to trying to find the girl whose face matches the one in the picture you gave me, well, it's not as easy as you might think. A lot of narrowing down. So far, I've found about eight different girls with pictures, somewhere along the line, who looked exactly like that. Even when I ran a facial recognition scan, the computer couldn't tell the difference."

Natalie's spirits are sinking faster than the level of wine left in the bottle. "But surely, there must be some other way of figuring out which one was at the hotel?"

"I was just coming to that. You see, they change frequently, but of course, they keep meticulous records of who was changing into what, exactly when, exactly where, you name it. The one thing I haven't yet been able to crack is their appointment scheduling. It seems almost like they keep that a secret even from themselves. Of course, when you're dealing with a clientele of the rich and famous, among other things, you obviously want as little chance of your appointments being crashed as possible. And that brings me to my final point. You see, at the time of Senator Bergman's mishap, there were two girls in the system who looked exactly like the girl in the picture. That's as far as I've gotten."

Natalie's heart jumps into her mouth, and she has to choke past it to get her words out. "Have you done the background on the girls in question?"

"As a matter of fact, I have." Alan suddenly sounds smug, not because he understands the importance of the fact, but because she was plainly worried that he hadn't. "The names are Jenna Friedman and Alice Bell. At the time, Bell was using the name 'Cleopatra.' Friedman was styled as 'Atalanta.' Bell seems to have originally been a pale, dark-haired vampire lass, and Friedman was a mousy jock type."

"And … what about their personal histories?" she whispers.

"Let's see … Bell started out as a stripper. It seems she only ever wanted to work in the flesh trade. She got in trouble at school for sending racy pictures of herself to the boys. She was one of the few girls from Fantasies who'd already had work done by Larsen's before she started working for them. Her family had enough money, and she felt she needed to fill herself out to be a good stripper. So anyway, yeah, she becomes a stripper the day she turned eighteen, did that for five years, and got fired for giving some guy a blow job when she was supposed to be giving him a lap dance. She tried to go legitimate and became a Starbucks barista for about six months. She hated it, managed to become a bikini barista, and did that for another three years. She was twenty-six when she started with Fantasies. That was two years ago. There's nothing else worth reporting. A model employee, lots of clients, no complaints."

"What about the other one?"

"Friedman is a bit more interesting. Comes from a hardworking middle-class family, good girl, good grades in school, goes to college up in Bellingham, gets involved in the Socialist Alternative, among other things. Very passionate kind of girl, always railing about something or other, online, in public, you name it. Eventually she gets a job working for some political organization in Seattle, bunch of radicals, always shooting off their big mouths, getting everybody riled up. She has some sort of a falling out with the group leadership. Over what? Nobody seems to know. Basically, she disappears for two months—and then shows up again as a Fantasies employee. Started with them about six months ago. Not much else to tell. Not quite as highly rated as Bell. Gets in some minor trouble for failing to meet some of the specifications in one of her earliest fantasy sessions. Apparently not quite as good at her job as she could be."

Is that a puzzle piece I feel falling into place?

Through a suddenly dry mouth, Natalie says "Alan, I think we've found our girl. I want you to drop everything else and find this Jenna Friedman. Can you do that?"

"Shouldn't be too much trouble—not after what I've been through to find her."

"And … you said she was called 'Atalanta' by the agency? Was that her name, do you think, or did they come up with it?"

"I'm not sure. They change names almost as often as they change appearances. Although considering how long she'd been there, that was probably always her professional name. Seemed like a weird choice to me."

"A weird choice indeed. Well, thank you very much, Alan. I think this is a real breakthrough. I can assure you that you will receive a great deal of gratitude when this is over." Her stomach is ready to churn, but her voice is steady.

Unlike his. "Good, good to hear, Natalie. Well, uh, good night then." She can taste his sad tongue, moistening his lips at every pause.

When the airborne connection has been severed, she sits in silence, pondering, taking a sip of wine every now and then, not noticing the tang, head swirling with more than the alcohol, heading toward some kind of a reckoning.

Atalanta … fascinating name for an escort. Oddly appropriate, come to think of, considering the name of the organization. She cannot quite remember the story. Her father, a professor of the classics, he loved Greek and Roman mythology, he was always reading those stories to her when she was a girl. His idea of bedtime stories, almost.

Beyond the veil of loss, a mental image is building: the image of a bookshelf. Does she still have the book? No reason why she shouldn't. It's not one of the ones she would have given away. No, it's one of the ones she would have held onto for the sake of sentimentality, to hold onto him when he passed.

There it is. Sure enough, when she gets up to look for it, the title nearly leaps off the shelf at her, far easier than she would have expected.

An old Borders Classic edition, the name of the long-defunct chain emblazoned optimistically at the bottom of the spine, black on white, the lower third of the cover separated from the black of the upper two-thirds by a thin strip of red. At the top, on the front, and also on the spine, in elegant white Times New Roman, OVID (for all the world as though it were a regular Anglo name) and beneath it *Metamorphoses* (again, you would swear to God that the ancient Roman poet had submitted it to some ancient Roman printing press in exactly that font), and in the center, an approximately three-inch-square image of a detail of a Roman mural, depicting an orange-garbed female figure turned away from the viewer, her hand reaching toward a flowering plant of some kind, woman and plant together isolated against an unnervingly dark background.

It takes a bit of flipping but she finds it, the story of Hippomenes and Atalanta, characterized in the text as "Venus on Atalanta." The story of a princess so beloved by her father that he would not force her to marry against her will, a princess so fleet of foot that she swore she would only marry the man who could beat her in a footrace, a princess so cruel that all who failed to outrace her were sacrificed to the gods. The story of Hippomenes, who was appalled by the carnage until he saw Atalanta stripped naked for the race, upon which he understood the passion of the libation-suitors and took up the challenge, praying to Venus for help and rewarded by her with three golden apples with which to distract Atalanta and thereby win the race. The story of a caper conducted perfectly, that is until the successful suitor got so caught up in the pleasure of his triumph that he forgot to offer thanks to the goddess who had helped him, who in vengeance compelled the amorous couple to copulate in the temple of another, even more vengeful goddess. A goddess who, upon witnessing her place of worship subjected to desecration, retaliated by turning the couple into lions, driving them out into the wilderness to roar their lives away in the barren wastes.

If there was any doubt before, it has vanished by the time Natalie has finished reacquainting herself with the myth. She has found her girl.

★   ★   ★

In the dark pit of the night, in the dark pit of his den, Senator Bergman looks from the image on the face of his computer screen to the expression on the face of Terrence, itself illuminated by the blinding light.

"The time, I think, has come, my friend," the senator says quietly, a tinge of guilt creeping in from somewhere. The emotion has been haunting him ever since his meeting with the archbishop. "Time to entrust this to Edgars."

"You are confident that enough time has passed?"

"I wish I were more confident, but this scandal has not been losing momentum as quickly as I had hoped. Nor have other developments been as fruitful as I may have wished. The time has come to act."

"As you say, Senator. Whatever else, I am sure Edgars will know what to do."

"Oh, he will handle it to perfection. As for the Schroder woman …"

★   ★   ★

The fingers of fate are inky and black and beautiful.

Alan may have read that somewhere, or it may have simply occurred to him on his own in one of his more poetic moments.

The Latin girl in the video shrieks, wiggles, bounces, envelops . . .

Soft and hard, fat and thin, why must everything come in pairs?

You would think there would be a more complicated spectrum of things.

Why must the thread always run straight from the one to the opposite of the one? Why must there be so little in between?

The woman shrieks, shrieks again, a different word each time, both of them Spanish. Alan does not speak Spanish, but he thinks he understands.

She's saying, "This is real. I really am enjoying this!" Not like Natalie fucking Schroder, the journalist so important she can't even be troubled to pretend.

Alan wonders how it feels. Not for the man, for the girl. He wonders, he has often wondered, how it must feel to be a woman. Not always in a sexual way, but usually. What must it feel like? What hidden protrusions and cavities must a woman sense within herself when she feels the shaft of a man poking around inside her, searching, a blind man in a cave full of stalactites and stalagmites?

Maybe it feels like this. Like sitting on a couch, with a load in your pants, waiting for death. Maybe there is that same sense of dead weight, of wetness where no wetness should be. A sense of opposites united by their opposition, by that invisible thread that ties every last boring thing in this boring universe together.

The fingers of fate are inky and black and beautiful.

The fingers of fate are inky? And black? And beautiful?

Surely they must be. Black like shadows, like the shadows that press upon his red-rimmed eyes from every corner of the room.

"Inky" and "black" are contradictions. You might not think so, but they are. Black is the absence of color. Ink is thick and gelatinous, sticky, visceral, real, real in every way, real like this hooker's orgasms.

As for beautiful.

Beautiful, that's the one that fits the bill. Black is the most beautiful color. Ink is the most beautiful liquid. The color of knowledge. The knowledge that oblivion is peace and quiet. Black, the color of oblivion.

The fingers of fate are inky and black and beautiful.

The shadows are inky and black and beautiful.

Oblivion is inky and black and beautiful.

Beautiful.

★　★　★

"Natalie? Good, you're still here."

The journalist in question swivels around slowly to face her boss, boldly stationed, as ever, in the entrance to her subordinate's cubicle, the light of a Friday afternoon shining agonizingly across the harbor in the window-distorted distance.

"Surprise, surprise. Me working late on a Friday. Because I love it here."

"Listen, Natalie, I just wanted to say, I hope I haven't been too hard on you this past week. It's been a stressful time for all of us, and I know you're doing your best."

The condescension in that last word is what sparks Natalie to speak hurriedly. "I believe I've made a breakthrough, you know." She knew Karin wouldn't be pleased, but it was a coin toss what emotion would settle on her face instead.

The initial phase is bafflement. "A breakthrough?"

"Yes. I believe I've found out the girl's name. I'm still waiting on information regarding her whereabouts. She's an elusive character, but I'm feeling confident."

Karin struggles mightily to keep the growing displeasure out of her face. "Oh, well, that's good to hear. Well done, Natalie."

"Thank you, Karin."

The latter is spared the trouble of responding when Marla appears at her shoulder, a new expensive purse slung over her shoulder.

"Hi, Natalie! Ready to go, Karin?"

"I certainly am, Marla." She does not bother to keep the relief out of her voice. "Well, I hope this leads to great successes, Natalie. You must be the first person to ..."

Karin appears to have run out of steam; perhaps her stomach is churning with the burden of heaping so much insincere praise on her despised employee. She comes to a breathless halt and stands impotent for a moment, the gazes of Natalie and Marla both heavily weighing on her, until she coughs in discomfort and continues, "Well, anyway, excellent work, Natalie. I'm very curious to see where this leads. Have a good weekend."

"Yes. Have a good weekend, Natalie!"

"You girls too!" *Cunts.*

⋆   ⋆   ⋆

Her phone buzzes in her pocket when she is halfway home, past downtown, getting toward Northgate, crawling along I-5 in the near-sundown pallor.

Alan.

She glances around hurriedly, no cops to be seen in the vicinity. *Okay.*

"Hello?"

A deep, phlegmy breath rattles across the connection.

"Hello?" Why is her heart beating erratically all of a sudden?

Another deep, phlegmy breath rattles across the connection.

Increasingly, she doubts Alan could breathe like that even if he tried.

"Hello? Who the fuck is this?"

A third deep, phlegmy breath rattles across the connection. Then the screen flares at the edge of her vision. The call lasted fourteen seconds, it tells her.

Shit.

She is not sure which is pressing harder on her temples, guilt or fear, as she turns around at the next off-ramp, heading the other, equally slow way back into Seattle, red taillights beckoning like the demon eyes of the abyss.

She arrives outside Alan's building when half the disc of the sun is still visible above the ridge on the other side of Puget Sound—not that she can see it from where she is forced to parallel park, in the shadow of the brick immensity.

She is careful to check that the automatic pistol in her glove box is loaded and racked before she settles it in her coat pocket and gets out of the car.

The unbroken elevator, whose doors still bear Alan's prankster signs, rattles like the last breath of the dying as it carries Natalie up sixteen floors.

His door is closed but unlocked when she tries it, no light visible at the sliver beneath. She has one hand halfway in the loaded pocket as she tests the doorknob and finds it unlocked. She has her finger on the trigger of the still-concealed weapon as she slowly opens the door. In the pitch dark, she releases the knob and fumbles along the doorframe until she finds the light switch. She flicks it and glances around hurriedly in every direction, perceiving nothing except the usual carnage, no sign of a struggle.

And, as expected, no Alan.

Everywhere she goes in the apartment is bigger than she realized, never having been beyond the living room. She flicks on the lights in every room, and in every room, she finds more mess—more of the endless chaos that the living room alone was enough to imply—and nothing of the young man who made it so.

Her shoes crunch over bags of chips, plastic cases, all kinds of plastic things, tangled wires, gadgetry of another sort. There is no point in watching her step, not considering the nature of the glaring absence, also, of course, because if she were to watch her step, the search would take far too long.

She is on her way back out, too dazed to be wondering what she is going to do—whether to call the police, if not them, then who—when she notices his laptop, sitting square in the middle of the couch cushion that was his personal throne.

The neatness of its positioning is what convinces her that it is meant as a message. Meant to be inspected. Alan would never have left it there so primly. The rest of the apartment is psychological evidence of that. She picks it up, cradling it under her left arm, raising the screen with her right, feeling like a mother holding an infant. Maybe she should unbutton her blouse for it, as she did so many times for Alan—perhaps that would complete the ritual.

The screen is dark for one split instant, and then an image appears upon it like a screensaver, nothing more. Nothing she clicks can shake it. There is nothing to be done with the laptop save to look at this image, the image given by herself to Alan, given to her by Mr. Edgars: the image of the girl who called herself Atalanta, the girl wrapped in a towel, a towel that suddenly brings to mind a toga party and with that train of thought the myth, the original myth. She sees the connection now. The athletic girl does in fact look like an Atalanta, ready to drop that towel and make a run for it while all the astonished male observers in the hotel room and the hotel hallway gape at her naked perfection, terrified to chase after her for fear of the sacrificial knife. And yet that defiance is all in the body language, all in the heat–pinked body, the flush in her brown features. The look in her eyes, the look that Natalie could not read before now, it finally dawns upon her as the beginnings of fear, not an ordinary fear, that's why it has been so inscrutable, rather the very first stage of mortal fear, disbelief, denial, far worse than anything the police could represent, not fear of arrest, fear rather of what will happen if they let her go free.

Which, Natalie now remembers, is precisely what happened.

She sets the laptop down, back where it came from, feeling the eyes glaring at her from every side. The panic is rising and falling with every inhale and exhale, nothing to be done about it, which is the ultimate snare. Whichever way she turns, the eyes will be there, invisible in a mirror, never looking you in the eye, always digging away into the back of your head, not even the back of head, rather into the spine, that's where the chill arises, that must be where the icy rays connect.

She hastens out of the apartment, not daring to take the elevator, the thought of the confined space fills her suddenly with claustrophobia. Better to take the stairs, burn off some of this nervous energy, some of this growing terror, this mounting existential dread, the needles gouging into every inch of her skin.

Is that another set of footsteps behind her or an echo?

Only an echo. Nevertheless, she picks up the pace.

The apartment building feels deserted, though here and there she can see the lights underneath the doors. But would anyone hear her if she screamed? If they did, would they be allowed to live, their doorways not go dark?

Natalie reaches the street, panting like Atalanta at the end of that fateful race, the race after which her unfortunate suitor was not slaughtered. The race she lost, and not to be sacrificed to the gods, no, much worse, as it turned out, for both of them.

She slams the car door shut, hands trembling maddeningly as she fumbles the gun out of her pocket and places it back in the glove box. The engine roars to life when at last she has agitatedly gotten the key in the ignition and pressed down unnecessarily tightly on the gas pedal.

The night has fallen, and while there is still light and stars visible to the west, overhead a storm is mustering. *Oh, Seattle.*

She has just turned on her headlights when the gesture is matched, much more brightly, to her rear left.

She puts the car in gear, twists the steering wheel far to the left to get out without scratching the car parked in front of her, waiting for Mr. Bright to move on.

He does not. Someone behind him starts honking. The streets are as crowded as ever even at this hour of the evening. The cars in the other lane are still moving, dutifully slowly, now being joined by the cars behind the man in the sun chariot.

She cannot quite make out what kind of car it is. It's big and black, tinted windows, so no chance of making out the driver or any potential passengers either.

If I pulled out the gun and shot him, how likely is it that I would get caught? Hard to say. Also hard to say if those windows are bulletproof or not.

The headache is spiking. Nothing—*nothing*—is worse than being trapped waiting. Not even being chased by a lunatic with two suns on the front of his car.

All right, fuck it.

Natalie pulls out into the lane with a resounding squeal of tires, but she cannot go far before the tightness of the traffic, the abundance of stoplights, the pedestrians, and the motionlessness of the car originally a hundred feet in front of her forces her to come to a halt. It is far enough to confirm her suspicions. Mr. Headlights lets off the brake as soon as she is in front of him, keeping close, and not letting any other drivers squeeze in between them.

She tilts the rearview mirror away from her, as far as possible, and leans away from the side mirror at an uncomfortable angle to mitigate the glare.

All the same, the glow remains, and with it the dark promise.

The red light lasts just long enough for her to begin to contemplate the sheer *realness* of it all. *This is actually happening to me. It's the sort of thing you never think actually happens to anyone, even though it does. Even worse, now I'm one of them, one of those unfortunates, the type I write about dispassionately for a living.*

She takes a right when the light turns, as soon as she gets to the corner. A wave of pedestrians has yet to fully cross the sidewalk. *These Seattle assholes always take forever. They think they have all the time in the world.* Her horn blares and sends them scuttling as she bulls her way between them, shouts and screams arising alongside the rude gestures, the shocked expressions, no time to care.

As soon as she is past them, the crowd of street-crossers begins to converge in her wake, forced to disperse again as the big black vehicle with the solar flares barges in among them. The effort on its part to avoid flattening anyone, probably just to avoid trouble, not actually caring whether any of them live or die— she knows the feeling—is enough to buy her a few seconds.

She is heading west, downhill, toward Pike Place she realizes, about to run out of road, no chance of getting out of the busiest streets anytime soon. Fortunately this street, at least, is practically devoid of vehicles. The main thrust of traffic at this hour is southward and northward. Nobody is in the left-turn lane, and the light is yellow. She floors it. The light has just turned red when her wheels are still behind the white line, but who cares? She's going too fast to stop. The other light won't have time to change to green before she is through the intersection in any case, joining the southbound. Sure enough, she makes it just in time. The light turns green above her as she brakes with her ass still hanging out in the intersection, wondering how long it will take Bright Boy to show up.

A blue and white flashing flares up, and a siren neighs like a whinnying police horse.

Oh, shit!

He was sitting to her right, all along, next in line at the southbound red light, a short cop on a motorcycle. He revs the engine and putts up behind her, a mechanical crackling beginning to split the air.

A screeching of tires, and the policeman—and his motorcycle—disappear, deposited thirty feet away by a massive black car hurrying down the hill.

Perhaps Mr. Bright didn't mean to flatten the cop. In fact, considering the consideration he showed to the pedestrians, probably not. He probably got caught up in trying to beat the light and the perpendicular traffic before it started moving, before it had time to interject itself between him and his quarry.

Oh well, one less racist cocksucker in the world.

The traffic ahead of her starts moving, albeit slowly, and the big black car has come to a halt at an angle, seemingly uncertain of what to do. It is largely blocking the lanes, but a couple of cars are already edging their way around him, apparently as unconcerned as Natalie for the fate of the policeman, plugging up the void behind her, between her and her pursuer. A hesitant relief is already blossoming when she sees the blinding headlights moving again, but they are separated now by at least two cars.

So it continues, long past the tunnel that replaced the viaduct twenty years ago. Mr. Bright is getting farther and farther back, unable to regain his former closeness.

She is still in the vicinity of the viaduct when it begins to rain, and the downpour no doubt helps, especially with those tinted windows, turning everything into a gray and red blur.

The only problem is, once she is well past the tunnel, heading into south Seattle, she really doesn't know where she is. The Industrial District was never an easy place to navigate to begin with. It's easier than downtown, of course, but that never meant much in Seattle. The growth of another thousand businesses in the region in the past ten years has blocked up the spaces that used to be empty, expanding vertically when there was nowhere left to go horizontally, crisscrossed now by several additional light rails, and it is a simple matter to get lost.

Especially if one had any intention of getting back to the freeway, which, she senses, is no longer an option for her. They obviously know who she is and where she lives. The panic wants to rise again, and the gun is less comfort than ever—or perhaps more. She can't say she hasn't thought about using it now and then over the years.

She is never certain afterward how or why she found her way to the docks. You would think it would be more difficult, that there would be fences, security, locks, things to obstruct one from so easily reaching the compounds that line the water, where the ships come into port, where the orange cranes loom, where the warehouses stretch endlessly in every direction, it seems, except to the watery limits of the east.

Speaking of watery limits, the rain is pouring so thickly by the time she reaches the water that she almost drives into it, right over the edge of the dock. You would think that too would be impossible—you would think the edge of the dock would be blocked somehow—but apparently it's not.

She brings the car to a stop, watching the raindrops dance in the glow of her headlights, rushing away to puddle on the ground. Her tires must be at least an inch deep in water already. The rain is splashing up and rippling distinctly with every drop, filling up a lake in the middle of a desert. There is nothing to be seen to either side except concrete for hundreds of yards. There are buildings of some sort behind her; she has driven a gap between them, and disconcertingly close in front of her, is the Sound.

The windows are steaming up. She is sweating profusely, and the rain is warm. The car is warm, it is summer after all, and the air-conditioner does not seem to be working.

Natalie leaves the car running and the headlights on as she gets out, her mind blank, to stretch her legs.

The sound of massive tires churning the waters does not make her turn around as quickly as it should. Not even when the sound is accompanied by a flare of blinding white reflected in the puddling rain.

She finally looks to her left when she hears the driver door thumping shut, after the sound of the engine and the glare of the headlights have ceased.

A jovial African voice speaks up from the raincoat-clad figure now standing beside her in the drink. "Well, Miss Schroder, you've certainly given us a run for our money. You and your friend, the computer geek. But that car chase—now that was fun."

"You enjoy racing cars, Mr. Edgar? I wouldn't have thought. I thought you blacks had nothing but contempt for NASCAR."

"NASCAR is a bunch of cracker bullshit, you got that straight, but that was the genuine article back there. And running over that copper? Oh man, now I know how Judge Hartmann felt, getting those three vicious motherfuckers in his grasp."

Despite herself, Natalie finds herself joining in his chortling. The sound echoes across the wet concrete. How strange—the things that bring people together.

"Let's take a walk, shall we, Miss Schroder? I brought an umbrella."

She is already soaked just about to the bone, but she is grateful for the reprieve as they set off down the docks. The rain is falling heavy and straight, no wind, so it does not blow much in their faces as they move.

"Well, now, Miss Schroder, or may I call you Natalie?"

"For the time being, I would prefer Miss Schroder."

"Very well, then, Miss Schroder, I'll get right to the point. Have you given anymore thought to the proposal made to you by my colleague, Miss Hopkins?"

Colleague? I must not be as perceptive as I think I am.

"To be honest, no, I haven't. I have had, I guess, other things on my mind."

"Perfectly understandable. Working toward a deadline while waiting on a clueless boy to hack the most sophisticated computer system in the world is no idle matter. Still, that's by the by now, and we have some time on our hands. Why don't you give it some thought right now?"

"Maybe you could remind me what the offer was? My brain is, shall we say, kinda fuzzy at the moment."

"No problem whatsoever, my dear. The offer stands as such: You give up on investigating a certain employee of Fantasies Inc. and a certain well-known client of hers. In return, we admit you into our friendship, a mutually beneficial relationship in which your respected position in the field of journalism benefits us while our respected position in the field of human pleasuring benefits you even more directly."

"And what about Alan?" Later, she will be proud of having thought of him in this moment, even in the midst of mortal fear.

Darren Edgars sighs. "I was hoping we would come to that a bit later, but since you mention it now … it's a bit difficult to see now, in the dark, and with all this rain, but perhaps you espy a shape, about two points starboard, standing at the very edge of the dock, about fifty yards off?"

Natalie squints and squints, and at length, she makes out one unmoving blotch of darkness amid the more protean blotches of darkness all about.

She is about to ask Edgars what it means, but he holds up a hand, insistently sloshing through the darkness in silence, until they come upon it.

Mr. Edgars wordlessly hands her the umbrella when they are perhaps five yards from the figure, standing unnaturally still, staring out to sea, the right height, the right build, but completely dark, devoid of nuance. She takes the wooden handle between her soaking fingers, steps closer, reaches out her other hand, and touches bronze. *What on earth is this? It is literally a statue.*

She edges her way around it, not certain what she is hoping to find or hoping not to find, and finds herself looking into a bronze face that certainly looks like Alan's, but exaggerated, distorted, perhaps simply to prove that they did not merely pour bronze all over his carcass and prop him up as a statue. The mouth, the lips are too wide, the nose too flared, the eyes too round and bulging to be even plausibly human. They actually made a statue of him, for whatever reason, and put it here, to make her wonder why, to send this tremor of revulsion through her, no other reason.

Natalie curses the stammer in her voice, edges back away from the metal imitation of flesh, and looks back at Edgars. "What did you do with him? Is he still alive?"

"He is alive and well, better, in fact, than he would have been if things had worked out as you intended. Which is but one of the reasons why you will never see him again. We at Fantasies are not unreasonable, Miss Schroder. We are not the bloodthirsty CIA, as your friend so paranoiacally assumed at one point. We have a good eye for talent; that is how we make our living. When we caught up with Alan, we merely made him an offer, rather like the one we are extending to you. He was a bit hastier in making up his mind. Who can blame him?"

That is plainly as comforting an answer as she is ever going to receive. So she nods, with as much gratitude as she can muster, and hands the umbrella back to him.

Hoisting it resolutely over their heads, he says, "Now that we've got that settled, we have one last order of business to attend to. You may have made up your mind already, but it is the wish of Miss Hopkins and myself that you fully understand what you are getting into before we hear your final decision. This way, if you please."

The oasis of dryness under the umbrella floats like a balloon toward the warehouse a hundred yards behind the statue, plain, gray, utilitarian in the rain.

Natalie remains in the rain as the umbrella moves past her.

Darren Edgars is perhaps ten feet away when he stops and turns to look back at her. "You know you are coming, Miss Schroder. We both know it."

"We both know it …" she mutters, rain dripping from the end of her nose as she nods. "You and Miss Hopkins know it. Mr. Edgars, who is Miss Hopkins? Tell me—or I will fuck you over somehow. I swear it."

His mouth twists in a mixture of amusement and respect. "I would answer your question if there was an answer, Miss Schroder. I promise you, I would.

The closest thing to an answer is this: Erin Hopkins is whoever I need her to be. Erin Hopkins is my greatest persona, so clever I could not keep her contained within myself. She is herself, as much a part of me as I am of her. But I created her—not the other way around."

He lifts the umbrella higher, invitingly, and Natalie joins him under it, not expecting any more explanation, and they proceed toward the warehouse in silence.

A ten-foot, paint-chipped red door rumbles upward when they are thirty feet away. There is no sign of anyone inside the bright space beyond. The spacious room is unoccupied by merchandise or human life of any apparent sort. *Is it some kind of electronic trigger—or some more mysterious chicanery?*

Concrete floor, row upon row of vast industrial light diluting the place from above, shelves and racks, unoccupied, a considerable distance away in every direction, hiding the walls, but the overwhelming impression is one of emptiness.

Except for the chair, the small but elegant chintz armchair, mahogany and red silk, situated precisely in the center of the plain gray floor.

"Right there, Miss Schroder, if you would have a seat," says Edgars, umbrella still unfurled, indicating with his other hand.

She cannot budge, not quite yet. "Mr. Edgars …" she begins slowly, knowing she is pushing her luck. "My mind is indeed made up. To make an ultimatum: I am perfectly prepared to accept your offer, if you can, if you will, tell me what happened at the Seashell Hotel that night. And what happened ... what happened to Atalanta."

He flinches, almost invisibly, but she is attuned to him now, and she catches the discrepancy before he turns his calm, fearsomely wise eyes upon her, as though seeing her in a way he had not seen before.

"Very well, Miss Schroder," he says at last. "That seems reasonable. Well played, if I do say so."

He coughs to himself, turns his gaze away, twirls the umbrella in his grip, humming, moving his chin up and down.

"The girl Atalanta," he begins without preamble, eyes fixed on the chintz chair, "or, as you now know her true name to have been, Jenna Fulbright, was a charming young woman, the sort of girl Fantasies relies on, clever, beautiful, willing, tough within and without, adaptable.

"But she was a troublemaker by nature. Everyone has a fatal flaw, some more fatal than others. I suppose the fatalism of the flaw depends on the circumstances, like everything else. Anyway. That was her fatal flaw, earning her a place in the Greek tragedy of her tragic little life.

"Personally, I always suspected she was up to no good. The way she came to us when she had nowhere else to turn—because her fellow political radicals weren't broad-minded enough for her. You can never trust a person like that. But certain of my colleagues were unconvinced by my warnings. Even in an organization specializing in knowing, in knowing *everything*, there is no excising human error. Some men, it seems, no matter how high they rise in the world by reading others, by being unswayed by the lesser, the simpler temptations, can yet be seduced by an innocent face and wide eyes, especially when they are paired with such a muscularly tender body."

Edgars snorts with contempt, hands no longer twirling but rather twisting furiously on the handle of the umbrella. "Well, they got what they paid for, as men inevitably do. Oh, and women too, of course, though if you'll forgive what some would no doubt call chauvinism, it sometimes seems that women are more inclined to think they can return the goods after the warranty has expired. I say so merely because that was what 'Atalanta' seemed to think she could get away with.

"She was not exactly what one would call a 'model employee' to begin with, though that is no great fault in itself. Sometimes, in this business, as in every other, people learn at different rates. Sometimes the ones who need reprimanding at first turn into the most skilled and loyal down the road. But this girl … she learned her lesson too quickly, it seemed to me. I could see the lingering defiance in her submission. Altogether too absolute, too obsequious to be sincere. Everyone else was fooled.

"Until, that is, she felt the need to try to photograph herself in bed with Senator Milton Bergman, which would have been bad enough, of course, even if she hadn't gotten herself caught in the act, prompting the senator to assail her, to smash her phone, and generally make a public nuisance of himself.

"What motivated her to do it? Your guess is as good as mine. I never got the chance to ask her. I will say, she did a fine job of disappearing for a while, after I told the police to let her get away from the hotel unmolested. Usually it is not so difficult for us to find people. Usually they feel the need to contact someone, alert someone, at the very least, even if they don't take refuge with them. Someone we can predict, keep an eye on, from their information. But this girl, she did a fine job of cutting herself loose. She understood the trouble she was in. If she hadn't gotten held up in Yakima …

"But I digress. As I say, what motivated her, I cannot possibly imagine. I could not believe someone who seemed so intelligent could be so foolish. Did she intend to blackmail him? Or us? Was it simply that he was a Republican? Was that too much for her proud college liberal soul to bear? Was it simply to disgrace him, to show the world what he is, pure political alacrity? Who can say. And now we'll never know."

There is, at least, a note of regret, of some kind of sadness, in his voice. He appears to have run out of energy for the recollecting.

Yet Natalie needs one last clarification. "You said … you mentioned that she, um, got held up in Yakima?"

He inhales with an unexpected shudder. "Yes. Yes, she was desperate for money of course. We emptied her bank account the moment we saw what had happened.

I called them from the hotel—she was probably not even out of the building when she went bankrupt. So, yes, she got caught offering herself to a fellow in a convenience store. He called the cops, thinking—correctly, I suppose—that she was soliciting, and so she found herself back on the radar. Hell, maybe she was hoping to get arrested. She would have been safer from us in prison, that's for sure. But they let her off the charge after a few days—not enough evidence—and we knew exactly where she was. Our boys were on her ass the moment she left the penitentiary."

Natalie almost whispers, "How *exactly* did they kill her?"

He actually chuckles. "As for that, even I do not know. There are things no one needs to know, and the secret to getting to the top is knowing what you need to know and what you don't. Saves room for the important things. You know."

She does, and she knows he is lying about not knowing how the girl died, and that she is never going to know. When he gestures toward the chair again, she sighs, resigned, and takes that hardest step forward.

She feels his eyes on her back all the way to the chair, but when she turns around to take a seat in it, he is gone, vanished into the shadows that are rapidly gathering as the lights are switched off, all save the one directly over her head.

Out of the darkness comes a repetitious tapping, the sound of footsteps, seemingly from somewhere up above, though she saw no walkways. The sound grows nearer, too rapidly it seems, there comes the rattle of solid soles on metal, coming down a metal stairway, and then slapping more forlornly across the cement, from her left, from behind her, it sounds like, until it oscillates, heading toward her line of vision, somehow she senses that she is not meant to move, not even her head, as the steps approach, the sound of high heels, stilettos in fact, approaching visibility.

Her body's reaction angers her. How can she be so suggestible? The desire is already spreading between her legs, in her nipples, in the palms clasped chastely on her knees. Her thighs are tingling. It would be humiliating if she weren't so angry.

And now here she comes, out of the darkness, a vague impression in the shadows long before the light falls on her: Erin Hopkins. She looks exactly as Natalie has longed to see her so many times in the brief period since they met, and so much more terrible, so immense, so penetrating in every aspect.

It occurs to Natalie that Erin is exactly the same height as Alan. The thought sends a swoop of disgust through her stomach. The nausea deepens. So does the excitement.

The big woman comes to halt with a yard to spare, staring deep into Natalie's eyes, alight with challenge, and this time, she meets the stare with relish. There is nothing left of which to be afraid. Only more pain.

"Do you still have the card I gave you?" Erin asks her, bluntly, not angrily, not pleasantly, simply forthrightly.

"Yes," she says in the same tone. "It's in my left pants pocket. In front."

Erin steps up close and bends down to pull it out, her breasts falling across Natalie's shoulder, their knees touching, as she reaches almost violently into her pocket and pulls out what she is looking for. When she has gotten it out, she turns it over and over in her grasp before finally tossing it aside. "Good girl. Now get on your knees."

Natalie obliges without hesitating. The other woman steps up close, looming like a fleshy mountain.

She is already gagging, fighting down vomit when Erin kicks her. Draws her knee back and brings the tip of her high-heeled toe crashing into Natalie's ribs.

The first kick leaves her winded, heaving. The second one takes her in the stomach, doubling her over. The third lays her out flat on her back, nothing broken, nothing bleeding, completely beaten, gasping for air, on the verge of tears.

There is nothing then, as the other woman descends upon her and envelops her, except a sort of fleshy blankness, impossible to comprehend, she is too far from consciousness. A massive weight seems to press upon her from every direction, accompanied by a stench that recalls the ocean, a sea of marine life mercilessly slaughtered, this is how she is engulfed. The pain is unbearable, and in it there is an unspeakable relief.

Her consciousness fades at the same moment everything explodes.

★   ★   ★

When Natalie comes to, she finds herself staring at the well-lit ceiling of the warehouse, no longer illuminated by the one light. Her ribs and midriff are still bruised, and her temples are pounding as though determined to burst, but the circulation has returned to her limbs. It hurts to move, but she manages easily enough.

The rain is still pouring outside, and the night has grown darker. She makes her way toward the large square exit. She hears footsteps coming from her right but pays them no heed until she is practically in the rain again.

"I hope you enjoyed yourself, Miss Schroder, and I look forward to collaborating with you in the near future," says the voice of Darren Edgars.

She comes to a halt but makes no reply, waiting for him to continue.

"When you get home, you will find an email from me, forwarded to me from the office of Senator Bergman. The contents will, I believe, be more than enough to make up for the story you were intending to print. And in case you're worried about your boss's reaction, I assure you, the fragrant Miss Karin will never trouble you again."

Natalie knows she should make some sort of response, but her mind is blank. She nods her gratitude and steps out into the rain.

"I apologize if it seems we have deprived you of the illusion of freedom," he says as she steps out into the night. "But don't worry—you would have lost it sooner or later. Everyone does, in the end."

★　★　★

Senator Bergman's library is all but pitch-black, illuminated only by a single lamp situated on a circular mahogany table, casting its witch light over leather book spines, hardwood flooring, and of course, the prematurely lined face of the senator.

"Please, take a seat, Miss Schroder," he begins, indicating the uncannily familiar chintz armchair opposite his own. "It's a pleasure to finally meet you one-on-one and not in a press conference."

"Thank you, Senator," she replies, taking the seat proffered.

"Before we go any further, Miss Schroder, there is a certain protocol I must outline. I hope I don't seem unnecessarily brusque or overbearing when I say this, but as we are going to be seeing quite a bit of each other for the foreseeable future, it is essential that certain forms be realized."

"Very well, Senator," Natalie mutters, apprehensive, intrigued.

Bergman steeples his fingertips under his chin and continues with the same polite condescension. "First of all, you must never ask me any questions, save clarifying questions, and even then, do not expect me to answer. I will provide you with all the information I feel you need to know. Is that acceptable to you, Miss Schroder?"

"It certainly is, Senator. I've learned there are things I'm happier not knowing."

"Dealing with the powerful can have that effect on the inquisitive. Which brings me to my second point." His voice changes, somehow, indefinably—only later will she register the tone as conspiratorial. "You must never expect me to tell you anything. For instance, you must never assume that I know anything about your friend Mr. Golding, who asked his sister to pretend to be the fretful Miss Mortmain on that pier at the request of Mr. Twombly, who is currently paying for his indiscretion with a suspension of his pension check. Or for that matter about the pitiable Miss Mortmain, recently awakened from her coma, albeit showing signs of severe memory loss. Likely just as well for her as for us."

Natalie cannot quite read the expression in his eyes as he cocks an eyebrow and twists his mouth. There is definitely a trace of pity, however. And shame.

"That is … good to know, Senator," she says, sounding raspy. "I understand."

He claps his hands together gently. "Excellent, Miss Schroder, excellent. By the way, Miss Schroder, do you know why I like to light my library only with this lamp? It reminds me of my favorite Gospel verse. Can you guess?"

Natalie looks him square in the eye and says, "'The light shines in the darkness, and the darkness has not overcome it.'"

The senator looks mildly impressed. "Very good, Miss Schroder, very good. Are you a Christian?"

"No, I am not a Christian."

"Are you a Democrat?"

"Define *Democrat*."

"Are you a lesbian?"

"Define *lesbian*."

"What exactly are you, Miss Schroder?"

"I am myself, Senator."

He sits back in his armchair, smiling, nodding. "Ms. Schroder, I think we are going to get along famously. I prefer to work with people who are not too much like myself. I find it fosters a certain … productive friction."

"Does it hurt my case that we have that in common?"

He laughs aloud. "I do have one further point to clarify, if you don't mind, Miss Schroder. I have followed your writing for some time now and, though you may not quite be a Democrat, you are certainly no Republican. I gather you are not a fan of my official positions on such matters as the arms bill and the SODO 3. How do you intend to reconcile these dispositions with our new … allegiance?"

She stares into his gray eyes long and hard. "Senator … there is no need for me to reconcile anything. I am not strong enough to care. These things are beyond my power to influence."

Bergman nods, slowly. "Ms. Schroder, I feel I need to come clean with you. I sense that you rather like me, almost in spite of yourself—rather how I feel about you. Here is why: I am as much a Republican as you are a Democrat. If I lived in a Republican state, I would be a Democrat. Like you, I cannot fit in with those around me. I need to be different. God gave me this need to be different. I believe the world needs people who need to be different. The world needs dissenters. Because no tyranny is good—not even the tyranny of a good idea. The only thing worse than a bad idea is no ideas. When there is no thought, everything dies. That is my comfort when I reflect on my need to dissent. I suspect you know what I mean. Am I correct?"

"You are so correct, Senator. I could not have put it better myself."

He leans forward and squeezes her elbow, eyes twinkling in the lamplight. "We are going to build a brave new world together, Miss Schroder. I am certain of it." He sits back. "Have you ever had a religious experience, Miss Schroder?"

She tenses at the weight of the question from this religious man. "Yes, I have."

He cocks an eyebrow again, looking mildly skeptical. "Tell me about it, please."

She takes a deep breath. It is a story she has never told before. And yet has. "It was my last year of college. Last quarter. My roommate, one of her friends, he invited us to a party. He said it was a tradition of one of the fraternities: 'the Ritual.' Part of the custom was the girls had to show up blindfolded. Of course, they didn't mention this until we were in the car. I was scared out of my mind, but my roommate, she'd known this guy, and his friends, for years, so she calmed me down and put the ribbon over my eyes. We drove for hours, it felt like. I still don't know where they actually took us."

Natalie chuckles now, nervously, quelling her mounting heartbeat. "I remember getting out of the car and walking up a bunch of rickety stairs, down a hall so thin I could feel both my arms bumping the walls, and then down some more rickety stairs into a basement." She sighs, hearing her throat rattle. "When they took the blindfolds off, the boys, there were a dozen boys standing naked around a pentagram. Red candles everywhere, some kind of Latin chanting coming from the stereo. The girls were all over in one corner. We were the last to arrive. The boys who brought us, they got undressed and joined the circle, facing the pentagram. Then this girl appeared from somewhere, this huge girl, blonde hair down to her waist, completely naked, covered in sweat, she was glowing gold in the candlelight. She was beautiful. She told us to strip and join the circle, and we did, and then …" Her voice trails off into silence, as a memory too horrible to face even now bubbles up.

Eventually, she squeezes the words out. The arachnid shape that waited in the center of that circle, and everything that followed.

Bergman looks faintly ill but no less fascinated by the time she is done. "So that was, ahem, a religious experience?"

"It was transcendent. It convinced me that there really is such a thing as evil in the world. Evil is like everything else: it needs context to mean anything at all. So, as long as there is evil, there must be good as well. That's the thought that gives me hope when I question my own ... dissident tendencies."

The senator stares at her in silence for one long moment. Finally, he nods solemnly and leans forward to squeeze her elbow again.

"Thank you for sharing that story, Miss Schroder. It's not what I was expecting, but I know I can trust you now. That's all I was after."

There is not enough breath left in her throat for a response.

"Well, Miss Schroder, now that we understand each other, let us get to the true purpose of this meeting. Now that we are on the same side, you will be entrusted with information to which no other reporter will have access so quickly. Here's an example."

Bergman reaches over to the circular table and lifts the screen of a laptop that Natalie has not noticed before. Blinking at the bright light in the darkness, she leans forward and scans the screen even as it burns her eyes.

EPILOGUE

Seattle Super-Church Pastor
Resigns in Wake of Scandal
by Natalie Schroder
June 25, 20—

SEATTLE—In a public statement last
night, Pastor Bob Dill of the Great Western
Washington Church announced his resignation
as pastor/president of that church and from his
position on the Northwest Christian Pastors
Council.

This public statement was made less than
twenty-four hours after three photographs
surfaced, appearing to show the pastor engaged
in sexual intercourse with a male companion,
whom Dill has since admitted to have been a
sex worker with whom he became acquainted
during a mission trip to Southeast Asia.

"The Lord sees all, the Lord knows all, the Lord forgives all," said Pastor Dill in the course of his statement, "but the affairs of men require delicate handling. In this, I have fallen short, and now I must do my duty."

Amid general shock and disbelief, the voice of Senator Milton Bergman (R–WA) has rung out in unexpected support for his friend, until recently his spiritual leader, who so vocally called for the senator's resignation in the wake of the Seashell Hotel scandal.

"I always said, even if I committed the sins of which I have been accused, which I didn't," Senator Bergman explained, "I still would not feel that those sins warranted my resignation. And, contrary to what Pastor Bob has called me, I am not a hypocrite. There is no reason, so far as I can see, why he should resign, except that so many members of his congregation will be unhappy with him. He is a good man, and a good pastor, and all men fall short. He should be raised back to his feet, not downtrodden."

Others have been less forgiving of the super-church leader's behavior.

"Pastor Bob once told us that there is no worse tyranny than hypocrisy," said Pamela Warburton, a member of Dill's congregation, referring to the now-famous sermon in which Dill subversively denounced Senator Bergman. "He has proven the truth of that by his own actions. As he would say, 'Give to Caesar what is Caesar's.'"

A poll conducted last night by Gallop found that, of the six hundred GWWC members surveyed, 64 percent approved of Dill's decision to resign, 32 percent disagreed, and 4 percent were undecided.

Of those who supported the resignation, more than 50 percent stated that their primary concern was the homosexual nature of the insinuations. Bob Dill has long taken a moderate stance toward homosexuality, but a substantial portion of his congregation has always been of a more conservative Christian inclination.

On the other hand, nearly 40 percent of those supporting the resignation stated that their primary concern was more the extramarital nature of the tryst, given that the incident occurred less than five years ago, while Pastor Dill has been married for more than twenty years.

Among those who oppose the resignation, there is a general consensus along the lines of Senator Bergman's defense of Pastor Dill.

"Bob is only human," said Marge Thewlis, seventy-one, who went on to defend Dill's record on the grounds that "if we were all held to the standard that the pastor is holding himself to, we would all be doomed."

With regard to his marriage, Dill has stated that his wife has long been aware of the incident, and he denies that he is homosexual. "I am a heterosexual man who loves his wife. It was a moment of temptation, of human weakness, and a sin. Nothing more."

"SODO 3" Executed by Lethal Injection; Seattle Bubbling Cauldron
by Natalie Schroder
August 27, 20—

SEATTLE—After months of public debates, a firestorm of protests from every corner of the globe, after a seemingly uncountable barrage of threats, counter-threats, appeals, speeches, and tears, the infamous 'SODO 3' (Derek Fry, Jon Olsen, Kyle Bolt) were executed by lethal injection last night, in accordance with the sentence passed by Judge Lucan Hartmann.

In the four months since the passing of the sentence, which came after a month-long trial following the release of a video showing the three white police officers brutally beating and murdering a homeless man of African American descent, Governor Dolores Cole found herself on the receiving end of a tidal wave of requests to override the "heartless" sentence.

"This inhuman decision by an openly bigoted judge would be appalling enough without this shocking apathy on the part of the state," said Martin Claudio, a Bellevue-based men's-rights activists who ran for the office of mayor of Seattle last year and who has frequently been denounced as a far-right extremist, despite his rejection of this label.

Such appeals, however, had no discernible effect on Governor Cole, who openly stood by Judge Hartmann in the face of not only innumerable appeals but also against an overwhelming tide of threats, both violent and political, from anonymous and not-so-anonymous sources.

"If Governor Cole thinks we are going to forget this, she could not be more mistaken," stated former Seattle Chief of Police Grace Howitzer, who resigned as soon as the fact of the execution was announced last night.

The decision was also denounced, predictably, by a wide range of pro-life figures and other activists, everyone from anti-capital punishment lobbyists to conventionally natalist institutions such as the Catholic Church, with many describing the actions of the judge and the governor as hypocritical, totalitarian, and unethical.

"You cannot prevent evil by doing evil," said Archbishop Luke Bouvier of Seattle. "That is the first rule, and Governor Cole especially, as a Catholic, should know that."

Nor was Archbishop Bouvier the only leading cleric to take a stand against the decision. Christian clergy, especially Catholics, have been calling in from all over the world to protest the sentence, including Pope Sylvester IV himself, who described Governor Coles inaction as "a truly shockingly uncharitable failure of the Christian conscience, and possible grounds for excommunication."

Meanwhile, the political repercussions for Governor Cole could be even more serious than those leveled by her largely anti-death penalty lobbyists and voting base.

"If Governor Cole wants to turn Washington state into a bastion of defiance against American values and American decency, then she may have to be taught that actions have consequences," stated President McNeil Bohr, who had previously taken no public position on the issue and who, like most Republicans, has never been known as an opponent of capital punishment.

Of greater concern to some is the mounting anger from the conservative white minority in the Seattle area, from whom not only the vast majority of the threats leveled against Governor Cole and Judge Hartmann have been drawn, but who have also been implicated in the recent increase in the number of hate crimes reported within the city precincts and several other places in Washington state.

"I always had mixed feelings about the death sentence itself," said Allie Myrtle, an African American Seattle resident, "but what really scared me was the thought of how all the angry white people would react if they went through with it. Now it looks like those fears are coming true."

The most worrisome thing, Myrtle went on to say, is the attitude that has manifested itself among the largely white, male police force. So far, there has been no noticeable increase in incidences of police brutality, but Grace Howitzer's ominous remarks seem indicative of a rebellious sentiment among the police force that could prove, to say the least, problematic.

"If the police won't protect us from the hate-mongers, well, there's no telling what will happen. We have enough to worry about from them to begin with," concluded Myrtle.

Klara Hugo, a spokeswoman for the radical Seattle-based paramilitary organization Lesbians with Guns, has taken a rather different stance. "If the white male gun nuts want to teach anybody a lesson, they're going to find us an uncooperative classroom. If the police won't do anything, they're not the only ones who can."

Arms Bill Passes Senate along Party Lines; Tempers Mount
by Natalie Schroder
September 7, 20—

WASHINGTON—In a late-night vote last night, the much-debated arms bill passed the Upper House of Congress with a 50–50 tie between Republicans and Democrats broken by Vice President Arthur Lime in favor of the bill.

"This is an immense accomplishment for the Republican legislature, and we are confident that it will usher in a new era in national security and economic expansion," stated Lime, who was among the leading drafters and advocates of the arms bill.

Though the bill has been months in the making, many remain unsatisfied with its provisions, even among conservatives.

Washington congresswoman Carolyn Bulk, one of the few Republicans in the Lower House to vote against the bill (it passed with 221 votes for, 214 against), has stated that she will support any effort to repeal the bill. "It was bad enough that they cut the Democrats completely out of the drafting. They could not even be troubled to heed any Republican voice that was not 100 percent blindly supportive."

The arms bill, which critics say will all but completely destroy the welfare safety net for approximately thirty million low-income Americans and possibly undermine our constitutional safeguards against economic monopolies, has also been imperiled by a range of factors beyond the strictly political.

"When I heard that [Senator Milton] Bergman was definitely going to vote for the bill, that in itself was almost enough to turn me against it," said Senator Julia Camus, R–Illinois, referring to the controversial Washington senator's infamous hotel scandal earlier this year, which many felt should have prompted his resignation.

Senator Bergman, for his part, conceded in the wake of the vote that he might have resigned, not because of any truth in the scandalous claims (which he continues to deny) but because of the difficulties involved in continuing to play a positive role in office while the rumors persist, had it not been for the imminence of the vote.

"I simply couldn't resign knowing that my seat would almost certainly be filled by a Democrat, not with the arms bill still in the offing," Bergman explained.

Many, in the wake of the scandal, anticipated such an attitude, with some expecting the senator to resign in the immediate aftermath of the vote. This seems unlikely, however, now that the results are in and Bergman's potential resignation can no longer make much difference to the Democratic opposition.

"To have guaranteed the passing of this arms bill," Senator Bergman extolled, "has been the crowning legislative achievement of my life, and nothing will overshadow it."

Other political commentators have been less optimistic.

"With every major piece of legislation, there are problems, things that need to be fixed, and the process of amending always requires a higher level of cooperation than the initial passing of the bill," said Miles Tollhouse, president of the liberal think tank Citizens for Progress. "It is always easier to get behind vague ideas than specific terms, and this is what always trips up legislators."

With every Democrat in the House aligned against everything the bill represents and many Republicans already expressing divided feelings, any effort at amendment could be a delicate tightrope to tread.

"I'm honestly not sure how this thing is going to work out," admitted Senator William Scalding, R–Montana, who voted for the bill despite expressing grave doubts about the effects it could have on welfare. "There may well be some validity to the claims made by the critics, and if they are proven correct, we may be forced to revise this piece of legislation pretty heavily. Otherwise, there may be no choice but to repeal."

Republican majority whip Julius Fulbright has angrily denounced Scalding and other "wish-washers," as he calls them, affirming that he will not tolerate dissent among the ranks and that he is confident any amendments necessary will be dealt with in a "satisfactory" manner.

Democratic minority whip Deborah Schlink, on the other hand, has stated in no uncertain terms that her party intends to fight the arms bill to the death.

"What's going on in Seattle right now is nothing compared to what will happen all over America if this bill is instituted for any significant period of time," said Schlink, referring to the disorder currently engulfing Washington state's largest city in the aftermath of the executions of the so-called SODO 3. "If the Republicans are truly concerned about national security, they should contemplate the threat of revolution."

Senator Bergman Announces Resignation, Citing Ill Health
by Natalie Schroder
September 19, 20—

SEATTLE—Less than two weeks after playing a pivotal role in the passing of the game-changing arms bill, Senator Milton Bergman,

R–WA, has announced his intention to resign his office at the end of the year, revealing that he has stomach cancer and does not expect to live out the rest of his term.

"I have done my duty, and now I want to spend what remains of my days with my family and friends," said the fifty-four-year-old senator, who went on to reaffirm that his decision is entirely unrelated to the controversial "Seashell affair" earlier this year.

The announcement was greeted with jubilation by many Democrats, including Bergman's longtime rival Chloe Demetrio, D–WA, who has long been a leading advocate for Bergman's resignation.

"It is past time that we weeded out the last of these privileged hypocrites who were never fit for office in the first place," stated Demetrio bluntly.

Less enthused were certain members of the Republican legislature, still embattled over the arms bill, considering the improbability of a Washington senatorial seat being filled by another Republican. Disgraced former governor of Washington Jules Reich has already announced his intention to run for the seat as an Independent, while confirming his liberal opposition to the arms bill.

"If I succeed in stealing the majority away from the Republicans, the first thing I am going to do is dedicate my every waking moment to seeing that that atrocity is repealed," Reich firmly pronounced in a press conference yesterday.

Reich, who was impeached two years ago in the midst of a private scandal to rival that of Senator Bergman, may be an unpopular choice with the Democratic Party leadership, especially in his home state, but he remains popular with moderate-to-liberal voters and may be the opposition's best chance in a short-notice election.

Meanwhile, Bergman, whose reputation would seem to have weathered the storm of scandal, has drawn a mixed range of responses from nonpolitical figures in the aftermath of his announcement.

"I think it's the right thing for him to do," said Melvin Thors, a Seattle resident and formerly a supporter of Bergman. "He's done his best; now it's time to go."

Polls indicate that a majority of voters believe that despite his claims to the contrary, Senator Bergman's resignation is at least in part a result of his hotel scandal in May.

"He knows we're onto him. He knows he's always going to be a controversial figure in the Senate, making things unnecessarily difficult for his own party," said Brenda Fox, a spokeswoman for the Seattle Women's Alliance.

"I'd be surprised if the GOP leaders didn't secretly pressure him into it."

Perhaps the most unequivocal statement came from Bob Dill, former pastor of the Great Western Washington Church, a leading critic of his former parishioner Senator Bergman, who was among the first to call for the senator's resignation and whose own reputation was paradoxically destroyed mere weeks later by the release of illicit photos that showed the religious leader in a compromising position with a seventeen-year-old Southeast Asian male prostitute.

"Everything is as God wills it," stated Dill, who remains an active proponent for Christianity in Seattle and who recently released a memoir entitled *The Face of Despair*, which has been alternately regarded as an effort to reconcile his sexuality with his faith by some and a hypocritical attempt to disguise his arguably criminal behavior beneath a smoke screen of kitschy self-evaluation. "The hand of God will not be denied its vengeance. It falls on the great and the small alike. It has been dealt to me, as it has been dealt to many, and it will inevitably be dealt to all. [Senator] Milton Bergman is in the process of learning that the hard way."

Bergman, who left the GWWC in the aftermath of Pastor Dill's denunciations, has recently begun attending Sunday Mass regularly at Saint James Cathedral alongside his political rivals Dolores Cole and Chloe Demetrio, to their evident discomfort.

"It is not for me to judge Bergman's soul, but this development is almost enough to make me wonder about what God is willing to admit under his roof," said Cole.

Archbishop Luke Bouvier, who has spoken privately with Bergman concerning his new interest in the Catholic faith, offered perhaps the most concise evaluation of the senator's character: "Milton Bergman is a man. Like all of us, a dichotomy, a melting pot of good and bad. All men are sinners. For those who sincerely repent of their wrongdoings, the hand of God is infinitely loving and forgiving—no matter what they have done. For those who do not, the judgment of God awaits."

Printed in the United States
By Bookmasters